Credits

<table>
<tr><td>

Author
John M. Stater

Developers
Bill Webb

Producers
Bill Webb and Charles A. Wright

Editor
Dawn Fischer

Layout and Graphic Design
Charles A. Wright

Front Cover Art
MKUltra Studios

</td><td>

Interior Art
Rowena Aitken

Cartography
Robert Altbauer

Playtesters
Frog God Games Staff

Special Thanks
Bill Webb would like to thank Bob Bledsaw and
Bill Owen for inventing the original
hex crawl — the standard in wilderness
adventure and a lifetime of fun.

</td></tr>
</table>

FROG GOD GAMES

TOUGH
ADVENTURES
FOR TOUGH
PLAYERS

Table of Contents

Hex Crawl Chronicles

— The Pirate Coast —

By John M. Stater

In ancient times the Pirate Coast was home to a great civilization of stone giants. The stone giants maintained a wide-reaching kingdom of towns and villages. Despite their great size and power they relied on slaves taken from the primitive human tribes of the coast. In time, the stone giants grew lazy and decadent. When humanoids poured into the coastal lands, they gradually destroyed the stone giant kingdom. The stone giants were more powerful than the humanoids, but the humanoids were more numerous and they outbred the giants. Worse yet, the stone giants found themselves plagued by slave revolts. TThe humans of the coast founded their own kingdom on the island to the east. The humans came to be known as Bucranians for the bull skulls they used as standards. More than a century ago, the roving pirates of the White Island discovered the wealth of the Bucranians and began raiding their villages and towns. When the White Islands sank, many settled along the Pirate Coast and started making deeper and deeper raids into Bucrania, burning villages and carting away slaves from the old and lethargic kingdom.

The Pirate Coast consists of vast woodlands of walnut, hickory, sweetgum trees, populars, red oaks and loblolly pines. Beneath the mighty trees there are creepers, wild grapes and raspberries, goldenrods, wild roses, dropworts and sassafras. The coastal lowlands gradually rise into wooded hills and then the Aderumdoc Mountains, which divide the Pirate Coast from the Empire of the Northmen beyond.

These lands are sparsely inhabited, the stone giants having long ago retreating into the earth and the humanoids devastating themselves with constant, useless feuds. The dwarves of the mountains and the elves of the hills linger, but they no longer thrive. The Bucranians are a spent race, having grown as decadent as their former masters and met their match in the invading Sea Lords. Adventurers can probe deep into this wilderness in search of ancient secrets and almost virgin territory to settle.

The Pirate Coast is a hex-crawl, referring to the hex-shaped units that divide the map. Just as dungeon adventures take place on a gridded map, wilderness adventures can be conducted on a hex map, allowing players the freedom to decide where their characters roam and giving them the thrill of discovering the many places and people that have been placed on the map. This map represents a large area filled with numerous places to discover and explore, and can be used as a campaign area in its own right, or dropped into an existing campaign. Referees can place adventures they have purchased or devised on their own into empty hexes on the map.

Adventures in the Wilderness

The hexes on this map are 6 miles wide from one side to the other. In open country, adventurers should be able to see from one side of the hex to another. In wooded hexes, vision is much more restricted. Random encounters with monsters should be diced for each day and each night, with encounters occurring on the roll of 1-2 on 1d6. The exact monster (or monsters) encountered depends on the terrain through which the adventurers are traveling. Unlike dungeons, in which the monsters on the upper levels are usually less powerful than the monsters on deeper levels, wilderness encounters are quite variable in their challenge, and low level characters face death every time they step out of the confines of civilization. Well-traveled adventurers will discover, however, that settled lands are not as dangerous as the rugged wilderness.

Pirates

The Pirate Coast's nickname originated just about a century ago, when the Albians, or Sea Lords, moved in after escaping the sinking of their homeland in the east. The merchants who moved up the coast between the Spice Islands of the mechanical pashas and the frost giant kingdoms of Ultima Thule soon found themselves preyed upon by the galleys of the Sea Lords.

In the present era there are three great pirate fleets along the coast, each commanded by an infamous captain. All of the Sea Lords operate in swift galleasses with 40 oars worked by 200 rowers and three sails. Ships usually carry a company of heavy crossbowmen and a single, several large ballistae used as grapnels and a large cannon in the prow beneath the lion figurehead common to the Sea Lords.

The three great captains of the coast are:

Wilderness Random Monster Encounters

Roll	Mountains	Swamps	Hills & Woodlands	Sea
1	Black Bear (1d4)	Boggart (1d8)	Black Bear (1d4)	Giant Eagle (1d3)
2	Dwarf (2d10+20)	Ghoul (1d6)	Elf (1d12+20)	Giant Octopus (1)
3	Giant eagle (1d6)	Giant Dragonflies (2d6)	Giant Owl (1d4)	Harpies (1d6+4)
4	Goblin (3d10+30)	Goblin (3d10+30)	Goblin (3d10+30)	Merchant Ship
5	Hill giant (1d4)	Green Hag (1)	Hobgoblin (3d8+30)	Mermaids (1d6+3; follow ship for 1d4 days)
6	Hobgoblin (3d8+30)	Orc (3d6+40)	Orc (3d6+40)	Orcawere (1d3; see **Hex 2329**)
7	Ogre (2d4)	Shambling Mound (1)	Patrol (2d10+20)	Pirate Ship (see below)
8	Orc (3d6+40)	Stirges (2d4)	Treant (1d3)	Sharks (1d6+10; follow ship for 1d4 days)
9	Patrol (2d10+20)	Viper (1, always surprise)	Werewolf (1d3)	Tritons (1d6+3)
10	Wolf (2d6+10)	Will o wisp (2d4)	Wolf (2d6+10)	Warrior Nymphs (1d6+6; see **Hex 1518**)

Bonny Prince Andus: Andus is not really a prince, but he is the black sheep of a noble family. Andus commands a fleet of four vessels and 270 pirates. Andus has silvery-blond hair (a curled wig) and striking, violet eyes. He has bronzed skin with a melancholy streak. A gourmand, he is slowly becoming too large to fit through the doorways on his ships, and often camps on the deck of his flagship, *Black Plunder*, on a velvet couch, attended by four halflings in baggy, velvet trousers and striped shirts. Andus' other boats are the *Vile Falsehood*, the *Full-Throated Scream* and the *Sea Lord's Pride*. His four under-captains are cold-hearted **Eitian**, honest **Garic**, selfish anti-cleric **Ivoma** and straightforward **Osson**. Andus is based in Slakethirst **[Hex 1624]**.

Bonny Prince Andus: Andus is not really a prince, but he is the black sheep of a noble family. Andus commands a fleet of four vessels and 270 pirates. Andus has silvery-blond hair (a curled wig) and striking, violet eyes. He has bronzed skin with a melancholy streak. A gourmand, he is slowly becoming too large to fit through the doorways on his ships, and often camps on the deck of his flagship, *Black Plunder*, on a velvet couch, attended by four halflings in baggy, velvet trousers and striped shirts. Andus' other boats are the *Vile Falsehood*, the *Full-Throated Scream* and the *Sea Lord's Pride*. His three under-captains are cold-hearted Eitian, honest Garic, selfish anti-cleric Ivoma and straightforward Osson. Andus is based in Slakethirst [1624].

Bonny Prince Andus, Fighter Lvl 11: HP 47; AC 3 [16]; Save 4; CL/XP 11/1700, Special: Multiple attacks, parry. Chainmail, buckler, long sword, dagger.

Eitian: Fighter Lvl 7: HP 35; AC 5 [14]; Save 8; CL/XP 7/600, Special: Multiple attacks, parry. Ring armor, buckler, short sword, dagger.

Garic, Fighter Lvl 4: HP 16; AC 5 [14]; Save 11; CL/XP 4/120, Special: Multiple attacks, parry. Ring armor, buckler, short sword, dagger.

Ivoma, Cleric Lvl 12: HP 43; AC 3 [16]; Save 4 (2 vs. paralysis and poison); CL/XP 13/2300; Special: Banish undead, spells (4/4/4/4/4/1). Chainmail, shield, light mace.

Osson, Fighter Lvl 4: HP 6; AC 5 [14]; Save 11; CL/XP 4/120, Special: Multiple attacks, parry. Ring armor, buckler, short sword, dagger.

Randar the Red: Based in the town of Hofn [2513], Randar is a greedy man, thin and powerfully muscled, with coarse, red hair and amber eyes. Once a dock worker, he climbed the ladder of piracy with grit and determination. He commands two galleasses (the *Murder Most Foul* and the *Bloody Finger*), each with a crew of 90 pirates. Randar commands the *Bloody Finger* assisted by his first mate, Stran. Stran is a delicate man with a skill at arms completely belied by his dandy appearance. He is a taciturn, spiteful man who seems destined to betray his captain one day. His second ship, *Murder Most Foul*, is commanded by an elf fighter/magic-user called Leofwyn.

Randar the Red, Fighter Lvl 8: HP 34; AC 4 [15]; Save 7; CL/XP 8/800, Special: Multiple attacks, parry. Chainmail, short sword, dagger.

Stran, Fighter Lvl 6: HP 29; AC 5 [14]; Save 9; CL/XP 6/400, Special: Multiple attacks, parry. Ring armor, buckler, short sword, dagger.

Leofwyn, Elf Fighter/Magic-User Lvl 7: HP 21; AC 9 [10]; Save 8 (7 vs. spells); CL/XP 9/1100, Special: Darkvision 60 ft., find secret door on 4 in 6, immune to paralysis from ghouls, multiple attacks, parry, spells (4/3/2/1). Short sword, dagger, spellbook.

Ydence Longshanks: Ydence Longshanks is a fragile looking woman with tanned skin, a heart-shaped face and wide lips, wavy auburn hair and bright, lively green eyes. Longshanks and her wild and woolly crew is based in Amistie [1615], and fortunately brings in more wealth than they inflict in property damage. Ydence is a pleasant enough woman for a pirate, but one must always beware, as she is ruthless when a person stands in her way.

Ydence commands 200 pirates on three galleasses, *Albia's Roar*, *Ready Damnation* and *Black Manta*, her flagship. Her lieutenant Kerik commands the *Ready Damnation* and her paramour, a lazy rapscallion from the Spice Islands named Zaibhir, commands the *Albia's Roar*.

Ydence Longshanks, Fighter Lvl 10: HP 33; AC 7 [12]; Save 5; CL/XP 10/1400, Special: Multiple attacks, parry. Leather armor, short sword, hand axe.

Kerik, Fighter Lvl 7: HP 29; AC 6 [13]; Save 8; CL/XP 7/600, Special: Multiple attacks, parry. Leather armor, buckler, short sword, dagger.

Zaibhir, Magic-User Lvl 7: HP 13; AC 9 [10]; Save 9 (7 vs. spells); CL/XP 7/600; Special: Spells (4/3/2/1). Dagger, darts (7), spellbook.

Sea Lords

The Sea Lords, or Albians, came from across the Briny Sea to escape the sinking of their homeland, the White Islands. Most of the Sea Lords that escaped this cataclysm were men, the crews of ships. The early settlers suffered a distinct lack of women, giving rise to the taking of slaves among female humanoids of the Pirate Coast. For this reason, there are still a good many Sea Lords with goblin, orc or (if they are lucky) elf blood flowing through their veins.

The average Sea Lord has pale skin (or deeply tanned skin for the crews of their lion-prowed galleys), blond to auburn hair and eyes ranging from blue to gray. Men and women tend to be exceptionally tall, with a pleasant, rough demeanor. Sea Lords always have a tale to tell, and in taverns they tell these tales to the accompaniment of fiddles, mouth harps and percussion provided by stamping feet and by clanging walking sticks and cudgels on whatever surface is handy. Sea Lords dress in leather tricorne hats, padded doublets and baggy pants tucked into tasseled buskins. Sea Ladies wear long dresses covered by shawls and pile their braided hair atop their heads, holding it with wooden pins. Noble Sea Lords and Ladies wear necklaces of bronzed leaves from their old domains in the White Islands.

The Sea Lords worship Albia, the White Goddess who created them and kept them until the betrayal of her father, the Briny Sea. Albia is a goddess of perfection and purity, the gleam in her father's eye until he consumed her in a fit of pique. Her followers worship her as a distant ideal and, in truth, out of tradition more than anything else. Where some religions produce holy water, the priests of Albia produce holy powders. The first were taken from the chalk cliffs of the White Islands, but modern powders, kept in vials of glass or silver, are drawn from chalk outcroppings on the Pirate Coast.

Last Men

The so-called "Last Men" are a population of men and women who consider themselves the last true humans left in Namera. All other peoples are infected with chaos and thus "sub-men" in the eyes of the Last Men. The Last Men have olive skin and blond hair. They are emotionless, bland people, their lives ordered by their master, The Golden God, and by an ingrained herd mentality. The Last Men deal in fabrics, growing cotton and mulberry trees. Their factories contain mechanical looms controlled by a difference engine kept in a great, black citadel in their city-state, located to the south of the Pirate Coast. The difference engine speaks to the Last Men through an automaton, the Golden God. Dealing as they do in fabrics, the Last Men dress in heaps and layers of clothing, all of expensive and luxurious fabrics like damask silk and velour. True xenophobes, they fear corruption by others, but still send out traders in

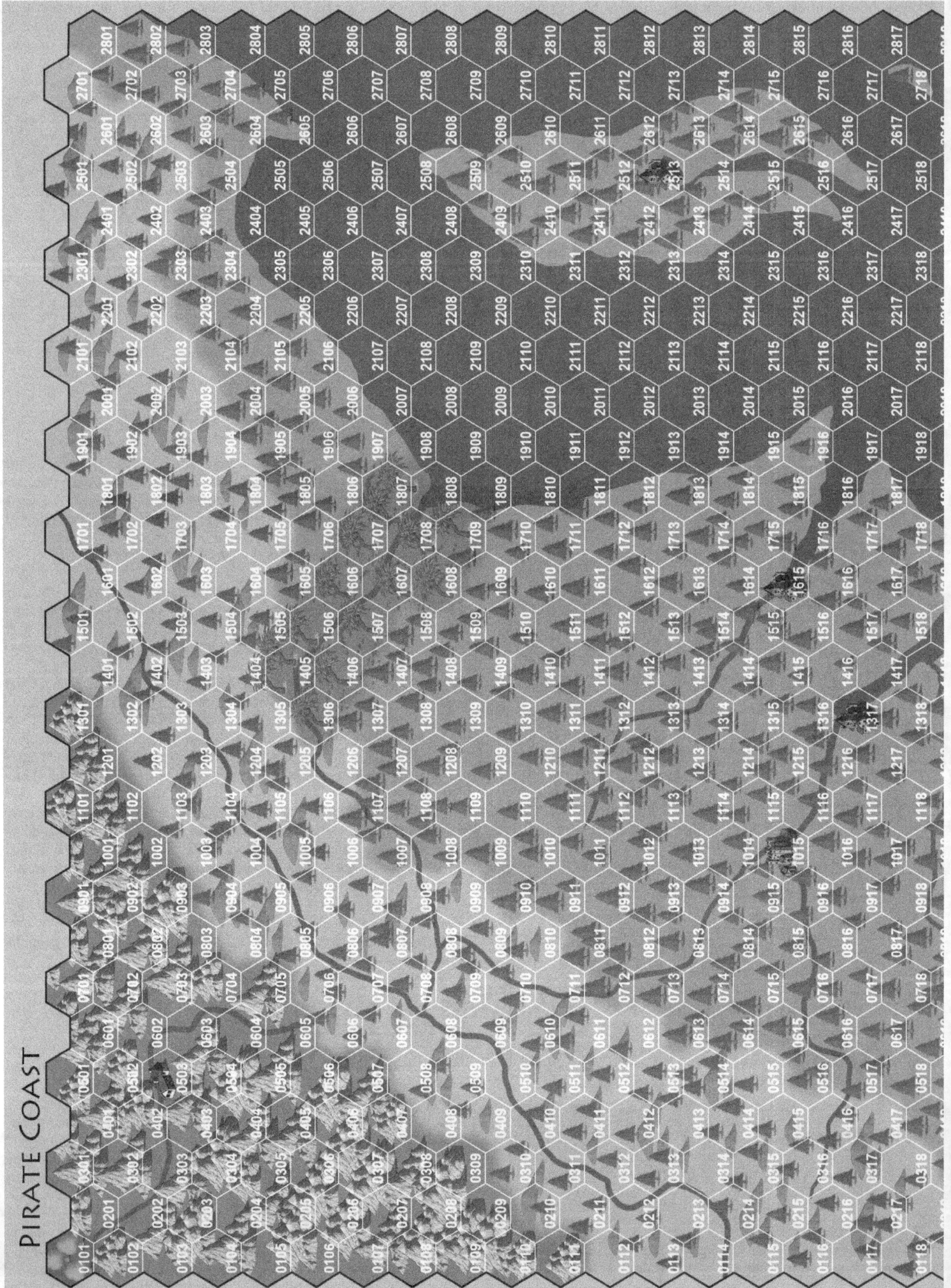
PIRATE COAST

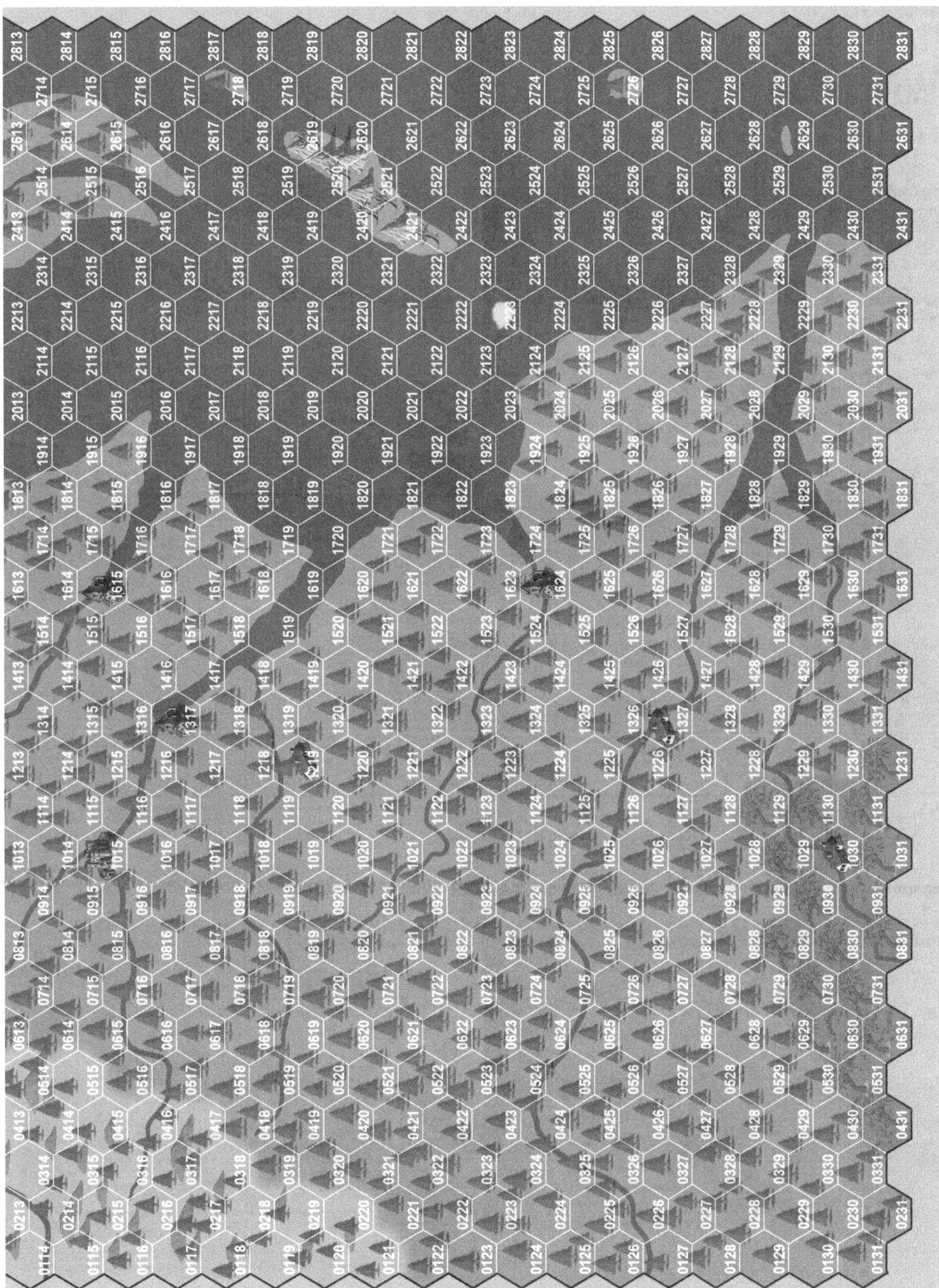

longships to trade fabrics for food and other items. Soldiers of the Last Men carry Bohemian ear-spoons (pole arms) and crossbows.

Bucranians

The Bucranians of the great island Bucrania are handsome folk, with chiseled physiques and deep olive skin. Their hair and eyes are as black as night. Bucrania is ruled by a hereditary king, called the Bull King. This man wears long, scarlet robes embroidered with silver and gold thread and a conical helm of brass fitted with the horns of a minotaur. Noble Bucranians dress in tunics of expensive fabric, most purchased from the Last Men, and square cloaks. They wear leather sandals on their feet and phetas of silk on their heads. Commoners dress as nobles, only with less expensive fabrics. Bucranian warriors wear ring mail armor and carry short swords, spears and scarlet, oblong shields embossed with black bulls.

In Bucrania, all women are wards of the king and live in one of his many palaces until they are wed to a man. The most valued men of the kingdom are athletes, and athletic games are frequent and hotly contested. Champions are adopted by the king and become princes of Bucrania. They are gathered into fraternal trios, and in these trios they battle minotaurs in the arena for the honor of their father and the favor of his "daughters".

Humanoids

The humanoids of the coast include goblins, orcs and hobgoblins. The goblins of the coast are naked savages, wearing nothing but loincloths and hide armor and carrying shields and clubs. They have wolfish muzzles with jutting fangs, beady eyes, long arms ending in clawed hands, stubby legs and long feet with prehensile toes.

The hobgoblins look like large goblins, with brightly colored skin and black hair. They dwell in hill forts composed of conical mud huts and dozens of bronze standards marking the different families. More civilized than the goblins, they wear checked cloaks over leather and ring armor and tend to carry large weapons like double-handed swords, battle axes and pole arms. The hobgoblins are metal workers, slave traders and herdsmen.

The orcs of the coast are cannibals and never to be trusted. They look like ashen-skinned, hunched men with squinty, yellow eyes, oversized canine teeth, swollen faces, pug noses and bald heads decorated with piercings. Orcs have large hands and bandy legs. They are swineherds and workers in bronze. Orc warriors paint their faces white and wear chainmail armor. They carry wide shields and arm themselves with axes and crossbows.

Elves

The elves of the Pirate Coast dwell in the wooded hills. They maintain hill forts like the hobgoblins, living in long houses. The elves are horsemen, raising herds of brilliant white horses. The elves veil their forts in illusions (*hallucinatory terrain*) to keep visitors away. Men and women wile away their days on great hunts through the woods, for the elves have exceedingly slow metabolisms and can support rather large populations on the slimmest rations. Elf warriors wear ornate armor and minimal clothing.

Dwarves

The dwarves have lived in the Aderumdoc Mountains since the time of the stone giants, digging their mines and halls and keeping away from the troubles of the surface. For generation after generation they have toiled beneath the earth, making war with the subterranean humanoids, occasionally leaving their halls to trade with stone giants and now humans. The dwarves are small and round, with grey skin that becomes covered by moss as they grow older and slower. The dwarves of the Aderumdocs are a patient, deliberate folk.

Rumors

When adventurers are seeking information or rumors in a settlement or from the lord of a castle, you can roll a random rumor from the table below. Each rumor is either True ("T") or False ("F") and the hex number associated with the rumor is given in brackets.

Roll	True Rumors	Roll	False Rumors
1	One would be wise to treat their horse with kindness **(Hex 0213)**	11	A wondrous secret lies behind a golden plate **(Hex 0131)**
2	Avoid the black brew of the goblins **(Hex 0223)**	12	Stone giants are deathly afraid of dogs
3	No good ever came from visiting Helltown in the Aderumdocs **(Hex 0503)**	13	Avoid the bearded stranger of the woods – his wink will steal your soul **(Hex 0610)**
4	A tribe of wealthy kobolds dwells in a cave lined with mother of pearl **(Hex 1006)**	14	Stories tell of a hawk-nosed god in the swamp whose drum raises the dead **(Hex 0721)**
5	Dudoga, the master of Fort Naomith, collects plants and pays well for specimens **(Hex 1015)**	15	Almar's women in Rogues' Harbor are glamered hags **(Hex 1030)**
6	Vaurock is up to no good **(Hex 1219)**	16	A satyr's etchings hold hidden magics **(Hex 1415)**
7	The Grey Vision wants to conquer the coast **(Hex 1812)**	17	Giant lynxes would be worthless if not for their pelts **(Hex 1901)**
8	The Pirate Coast is cursed – you can't even trust the sandbars **(Hex 1922)**	18	Acenn has a treasure hidden beneath the floor of her great hall **(Hex 2106)**
9	Mermaids claim a giant diamond rests at the bottom of the bay **(Hex 2120)**	19	They say the location of Blue Belly's treasure is marked by a light on the coast
10	A black candle is proof against an ill wind **(Hex 2125)**	20	Beneath the emotionless exterior of a Last Man beats a heart of pure gold **(Hex 2331)**

Encounter Key

OIO8.

The floor of this valley is a chain of shallow lakes linked by channels of sandy, sluggish streams. The lakes are heated geo-thermally, and this has made the valley steamy and verdant. In ages past, great creatures akin to reptiles lived in the valley until they were hunted to extinction by the ancient elves – many an old elven sword has a pommel wrapped in leather cured from their skin and ancient elf lodges often have their strange, massive heads mounted on the walls.

While these massive beasts no longer roam the valley, their spirits do, and are encountered here on a roll of 1-2 on 1d6 (1-4 on 1d6 during a full moon). Use the following table to determine what kind of animal is encountered.

1-3	**Ankylosaurus:** HD 8; AC 0 [19]; Atk 1 clubbed tail (special); Move 9; Save 8; CL/XP 8/800; Special: None.
4	**Brontosaurus:** HD 25; AC 6 [13]; Atk 1 stomp (special); Move 9; Save 3; CL/XP 25/5900; Special: None.
5-6	**Stegosaurus:** HD 15; AC 2 [17]; Atk 1 bite (special), 1 spiked tail (special); Move 9; Save 3; CL/XP 15/2900; Special: None.
7-8	**Triceratops:** HD 15; AC 0 [19] front, 5 [14] back; Atk 1 gore (special); Move 12; Save 3; CL/XP 15/2900; Special: None.
9-10	**Tyrannosaurus:** HD 18; AC 4 [15]; Atk 1 bite (special); Move 18; Save 3; CL/XP 19/2400; Special: Chews and tears.

The dinosaur spirits are ethereal, and can thus only be harmed by silver or magical weapons and spells of force or dispelling. Their attacks cause 2d6 points of chilling cold damage and force a victim to save or be drained of one level.

One of the shallow lakes is an illusion, hiding an ivory palace of the ancient elves – one that has been abandoned and forgotten for centuries. The palace is composed of eighty-one cells, each with a vaulted ceiling and connected to four adjacent vaults via a short (5 feet long) passage. These passages are blocked by walls of force, each one a shimmering curtain of one of five colors – cerise, ultramarine, gamboge, myrtle and heliotrope.

The palace has four entrances; each of these entrance cells has only three curtains of force blocking further access to the palace. One of these entrance cells contains a colored tetrahedron of metal, the exact color being determined randomly (see below). In the middle of each cell there is a tripedal stand which fits this tetrahedron. By placing the tetrahedron in the base and tapping it with something metallic, the corresponding colored curtain of force disappears for 1 minute. The colors of the curtains in each cell should be determined randomly with a d10 (1-2 = cerise, 3-4 = ultramarine; 5-6 = gamboge; 7-8 = myrtle; 9-10 = heliotrope), and the color of the tetrahedron changes (using the same random table) when it is brought into a new cell. This makes moving through the strange palace quite a chore, and potentially dangerous as there is a slight chance one will enter a cell and be unable to exit due to the color of the tetrahedron.

Each time a cell is entered, there is a 1 in 1d6 chance of a random monster (CL 3) appearing in the cell. These monsters are given the same random colors as the rooms and tetrahedron, and the color of the creature makes it vulnerable to a single form of attack: Cerise = cold, Ultramarine = fire; Gamboge = silver; Myrtle = steel and Heliotrope = wood. All of these beasts can be harmed by magic missiles. Their bodies disappear after one leaves their cell.

The center cells of the palace are combined into a single large chamber. In the middle of this chamber there is an elf-hewn idol of a four-faced, eight-armed and eight-legged goddess. Each pair of hands holds a golden plate hidden by a pelt of sable. The plates face the curtains of colored force, and these colors determine what secrets are etched on the plates.

The plate facing a cerise curtain is attuned to fighters (and rangers and paladins). The plate facing an ultramarine curtain is attuned to clerics (and druids). The plate facing a myrtle curtain is attuned to thieves (and assassins and monks) and the plate facing a gamboge curtain is attuned to magic-users. A plate facing a heliotrope curtain is replaced by a portal into the void, per a *sphere of annihilation.*

Looking upon a plate not attuned to their class forces a character to save vs. blindness. Looking upon the proper plate grants a magic-user a new spell of their highest spell level (though it must be written into their spellbook), a cleric or druid access to a magic-user spell that can be associated with their deity, a fighter-type a +1 bonus to wield a random weapon and a thief-type a +10% bonus to use one of their skills.

OI2I.

Amidst a barren heath there is a wondrous, shimmering sword lying atop a stone table. The heath is fluttered over by thousands of red butterflies. Folk who enter the heath are attacked by these swarms (see below), which have the power to turn them into virtual zombies. The sword is protected by these zombies, of which there are currently twelve. Those invaders of the heath that cannot be controlled by the butterflies are instead captured by the zombies, who throw them into an abandoned silver mine. The mine is nothing more than a hole in the ground and a couple miles of passages that are now inhabited by green slimes. The sword is a relic of chaos, the finger of a primordial demon severed by an angel's sword and given the form of a shimmering blade of rainbow hued steel on the material plane. The sword is a *+1 weapon, +3 vs. lawful creatures* and capable of unleashing a blast of rainbow-colored energy in a radius of 30 feet once per week. All caught in this energy must pass a saving throw or have their ability scores randomly changed about – i.e. a wise man might become strong, a foolish man sickly.

Treat each butterfly swarm as a single creature.

Butterfly Swarms (5): HD 4; AC 4[15]; Atk 1 (special); Move 6; Save 13; AL N; CL/XP 8/800; Special: immune to weapons, damaged only by "area" spells, successful attack by swarm requires saving throw to avoid complete mental domination by the swarm.

OI3I.

A golden plate has been affixed to a hillside here. It is partially obscured by trees and rose vines. The plate, which measures about 3 feet in diameter, contains, in extreme miniature, a blueprint of the cosmos. The plate cannot easily be removed from the hillside. The act requires one to dispel magic, cast transmute rock to mud and then put about 30 points of strength to bear in prying it away. This reveals a portable hole that steams and smokes and allows a female pit fiend called Naronca to crawl into the Material Plane, intent on retrieving the plate. In the library of a magic-user, the plate can aid in researches into spells of teleportation and plane shifting.

Naronca: HD 13 (50 hp); AC -3 [24]; Atk 2 wings (1d4), 2 claws (1d6), bite (2d6 + poison) and tail (2d4 + constriction); Move 15 (F24); Save 3; CL/XP 23/5300; Special: Poison (save or die), tail constriction (saving throw or 2d4 damage per round until an open doors roll is made), regeneration 2 hp/rd, +3 or better weapon to hit, immune to fire and poison, resistance to cold (50%), magic resistance (50%), spells (animate dead, charm person, detect magic, detect invisibility, fireball, hold person, invisibility, phantasmal force, polymorph self, suggestion, teleport, wall of fire).

O2IO.

A covey of annis dwell here on a highland meadow where stands a toppled tower of the stone giants. All that remains of the tower is the ground floor, the walls of which stands anywhere from 10 to 15 feet in height and measure 60 feet in diameter. The light of their fire casts weird shadows on the meadow at night and thick mists cover the area around the ruined tower. The hags leave their dwelling at night in the form of wolves and owls, visiting the local humanoid tribes to cow their leaders into submission. The hags seek a dark champion they can use as a puppet to unite the humanoids and drive the Sea Lords from the Pirate Coast. The hags keep their treasure in a leather sack made from the head of a storm giant, the neck being sewn up and the bag accessed through the unfortunate creature's mouth. The treasure consists of 9 steel coins (each one forces a spirit to leave a body or an extraplanar creature to leave the material plane if it is pressed into their forehead), a lapis lazuli (worth 200 gp), a steel bracelet studded with carnelians (worth 300 gp), a three gilt short swords (worth 200 gp each).

Annis: HD 8; AC 1 [18]; Atk 2 claws (2d8), 1 bite (1d8); Move 12; Save 8; CL/XP 10/1400; Special: Hug and rend, polymorph, call mists.

0213.

The valleys here are thick with herds of horses – magnificent animals with chestnut coats and reddish-black manes. The valley is filled with rolling, undulating plains covered with grass and crossed by a multitude of rushing streams. The valley also contains a crude stone shrine to the Lord of Horses. The Lord often visits the valley, running with his children and luxuriating in the sweet grasses. There is a 1 in 20 chance he will be present in the valley when adventurers enter it, taking the form of a magnificent white stallion with a golden mane or the shape of a handsome man with a long face, porcelain skin and golden hair and wearing simple clothes and carrying an ancient staff of hickory. Centaurs often come down from the mountains to worship at the shrine, painting their faces with blue handprints. There is a 1 in 8 chance they will be present at the shrine when visited by adventurers.

Lord of Horses: HD 15 (88 hp); AC 2 [17]; Atk 2 strikes in human form (1d8+2) or 2 hooves (1d6+1) and bite (1d4+1) in horse form; Move 18; Save 3 (2 vs. spells); CL/XP 20/5000; Special: +1 or better weapon to hit, magic resistance (45%), command horses, summon 1d6+4 warhorses with max. hit points or 1d4+4 centaurs with max. hit points once per day, cast spells as 6th level druid.

0215.

The ground gives way to a deep depression here with sheer, cracked walls. The pit was a surface gold mine worked by dwarves long ago, until they released a strange creature from the stone and fled the site. The creature is a golden cloud about 20 feet in diameter whose touch coats a person in gold. Three of the dwarves lie here in this state, dead and coated in a layer about a quarter of an inch thick (and worth 3,000 gp each). The dwarves' angry spirits dwell within the gold shells as oblivion wraiths.

Gold Cloud: HD 8; AC 2 [17]; Atk 1 strike (2d8); Move (Fly 36); Save 8; CL/XP 9/1100; Special: Touch coats people with gold unless they save. A person coated suffocates in two minutes unless freed.

Oblivion Wraith: HD 12; AC 1 [18]; Atk 1 touch (3d6 + attribute drain); Move 15 (Fly 30); Save 3; CL/XP 14/2600; Special: Drain attributes, immune to non-magical weapons, disintegrates objects.

0218.

A large goblin tribe, the Gibbous Moon, dwells here in a sprawling village. The village houses 500 goblins in furry hide tents. Besides raiding and working as mercenaries for ne'er-do-wells, the goblins make a living as miners, pulling spinels out of the wasteland of limestone hills and steam vents that serves as their homeland. The goblins of the Gibbous Moon are ruled by Thorx, a large goblin with pale blue skin. Thorx is worshipped as a living god by his people. He is attended by three witch doctors, each capable of casting spells as a 2nd level cleric and a 1st level magic-user. The goblins are known for their disdain of strong emotions and their love of a black brew [0223] that puts them into sour, fatalistic moods.

0223.

A glistening black monument rises from a sloped plain of dead grasses and stones and massive salt outcroppings with vaguely humanoid shapes. Sangria-colored liquid oozes from the monument, forming uneven pools.

The outcroppings are all that remains of a stone giant army and they can be communicated with using *speak with dead*. They can tell the tale of a powerful demon, the bane of the stone giant kingdom, who was finally brought to heel here and destroyed by an army of stone giants. From its corpse came a surge of dark energy that turned the stone giants to salt; and from the demon's corpse the monument erupted. The liquid is not poisonous. In fact, it refreshes and strengthens, but causes one to become wanton and cruel. Goblins in the surrounding woodlands bottle it and sell it as fortified wine called black brew.

0228.

There is a gully here with a sluggish stream that flows from the hills into a tunnel embedded with crystals in the walls. The tunnel is a portal to other worlds, the destination being controlled by piping different tunes on a flute. A small college of bards knows the secret tunes. They wander throughout the countryside, but maintain a guild house of sorts in Slakethirst [1624] and charge a pretty penny to those who wish to use the tunnel. If adventurers look closely at these crystals they can see the reflections of people, some of them looking back knowingly.

0301.

The land here becomes gray and rocky. In its midst there is a kidney-shaped lake of placid water. The lake is dotted with a few small islands inhabited by brilliant chestnut and blue starlings. The lake supports a variety of aquatic life, as well as a lonely cambion called Nonndus. Nonndus is a tall, handsome man with red, scaly skin, golden eyes and small horns. He dwells on the lake, moving from island to island on a small barge, living off the fish he catches and starling eggs, avoiding civilization for fear that it will bring out his demonic urges. He keeps a treasure of 2,120 sp, 1,410 gp and a scroll containing two spells, *extension I* and *wall of ice*.

Nonndus the Cambion: HD 8 (32 hp); AC 1 [18]; Atk 1 weapon (1d8) or 2 claws (1d6); Move 15; Save 8; CL/XP 12/2000; Special: Spells (cause fear, ESP, levitate, polymorph self), +1 or better weapon to hit, immune to electricity and poison, magic resistance (20%), telepathy 100 ft.

0304.

The Stone-Bones dwarf tribe dwells here in a stone fastness with an ornate door of hickory bound in interlocking iron and bronze bands. The fastness is a doughty little fortress of cyclopean granite blocks surrounded by wooded ridges; the dwarves dwell beneath the fastness in cozy burrows hung with elaborate quilts that not only tell the story of their clans, but are also woven with protective runes, giving each burrow the benefit of a *protection from evil* spell. The fastness is defended by a brotherhood of warrior-priests, worshipers of "Their Mother's Bones", their term for the stone and rock of the world and their mother goddess. The dwarf priests maintain the local weather conditions and protect their tribe from the savage humanoids of the lowlands. The priests are commanded by Zwellaun, a gnarly old dwarf with an "evil eye" (actually a lost eye that has been replaced by a 50 gp opal) and droopy gray whiskers that match the gray of his skin. Like most dwarves of the Pirate Coast, he cultivates a fine sheen of moss on his body, giving him the appearance of aged gray-green stone and aiding him in hiding both in the woodlands atop the Aderumdoc Mountains and the tunnels that run beneath those mountains.

The Stone-Bones tribe makes a living felling timber and selling it down river. They are expert woodworkers and, like most dwarves, skilled in metalworking and stonecutting as well. They are severely lawful in their attitudes, despising frivolous pursuits like gambling and conducting every aspect of their lives with solemn ritual. The dwarves wear heavy woolens of muted browns and greens, with knee-length trousers and leather tunics over chemise. They wear leather gloves and kerchiefs over their heads.

Zwellaum, Dwarf Fighter/Cleric Lvl 6: HP 30; AC 1 [18]; Save 9 (8 vs. paralysis and poison, 5 vs. magic); CL/XP 8/800, Special: Note features of stonework, darkvision 60 ft., multiple attacks, parry, spells (2/2/1/1). Platemail, shield, war hammer, holy symbol.

0306.

Those entering this otherwise pleasant valley hear a terrible noise like the shrieking of a thousand harpies. The noise issues forth from a great engine crafted by the dwarves in the image of a shovel tusker (a prehistoric relative of the elephant) with drowsy eyes. The engine is about 20 feet long and 14 feet tall, with four wide legs with claws that dig into the ground and an extended jaw that digs into the earth. The soil and ore falls into the interior of the machine where it is sorted by a team of dwarves, their leader Orrack operating the machine. That which is rejected is dumped from the machine's neck to the ground below. The dwarves have cleared about 3 acres of land and discovered about 15 pounds of gold ore.

0309.

The tall granite cliffs here are a mere illusion, hiding a great manse of the stone giants. Once the masters of the coast and possessed of an advanced civilization, the stone giants have been reduced to a primitive state, though they retain some of their old power. The clan that lives in the caves that riddle these cliffs number 24 adults, seven gangly children, three cave bears and three elders called Cam, Muth and Oroc. The interior of the caves is decorated with cave paintings and carvings that harken back to the glorious civilization of the stone giants. Hidden in the caves are about 1,000 gp worth of pelts and hides, eight large clay vessels containing hard cider (60 gallons, 500 lb in each, worth 2 sp/gallon), a large crate containing jugs of molasses (10 jugs, 3 lb each, worth 30 gp each), 4 gp/1,270 sp, 11,630 gp and 500 pp, most of it in triple-sized discs stamped with images of vines and beetles – the coinage of the ancient stone giants.

Cave Bear: HD 7; AC 6 [13]; Atk 2 claws (1d6+1), 1 bite (1d10+1); Move 12; Save 9; CL/XP 7/600; Special: Hug.

Stone Giant: HD 9+3; AC 0 [19]; Atk 1 club (3d6); Move 12; Save 6; CL/XP 10/1400; Special: Throw boulders.

Elders: HD 9+3; AC 0 [19]; Atk 1 club (3d6); Move 12; Save 6; CL/XP 10/1400; Special: Throw boulders, cast spells as 6th level magic-users.

0411.

A lodge of three giant beavers has created a lake here behind a massive dam. The lake now covers a small hamlet of woodsmen who have had to retreat to Fort Naomith [1015]. The hamlet had a stone church with a cellar that contained a large, round crystal that apparently held the preserved eye of the demi-goddess Thian the Night, a queen among night hags long ago defeated in combat by the paladin Caoline. The orb has been stolen by sprites and is now held in their cave lair in the hills. The crystal acts as a crystal ball capable of possessing its user.

Sprite: HD 1d6; AC 4 [15]; Atk 1 short sword (1d3) or short bow (1d4); Move 12 (F24); Save 18; CL/XP 2/30; Special: Sleep arrows, speak with animals, spells (detect invisibility, invisibility (self)), magic resistance (25%).

0424.

The orcs of the Bleeding Eye tribe dwell on this floodplain, digging their lairs into rocky promontories. In all, there are three orc villages in the hex, each housing 1d4 x 100 orcs. Two of the villages are commanded by sub-chiefs with 4 HD while the third is commanded by the great chief Vilax, a canny old orc with 7 HD and a +1 throwing axe that inflicts double damage against plant creatures and splits small to medium sized trees when it hits them. The orcs keep vicious wolves as guard animals and for their hunts. They are expert metal workers, wearing ring armor and chainmail and carrying all manner of spears, axes and pole arms.

Vilax: HD 7 (30 hp); AC 1 [18]; Atk 1 weapon (1d8+1); Move 6; Save 9; CL/XP 7/600; Special: None. Platemail, battleaxe.

0426.

A small monastery of dark gray stone is inhabited by men known as the Bald Friars. The friars worship a leather-bound tome that purportedly contains a conversation between an angel and demon on the nature of the cosmos. The friars are staunchly neutral. They got their nickname by shaving their bodies of all hair, including eyebrows. They dye their bodies in vegetable dyes based upon their "level of enlightenment" within their religious community and wear leather armor under black, hooded robes. The monastery contains a courtyard that is a natural cranberry bog decorated with weathered wooden totems bearing angel and demon shapes sticking out of the water, as well as wooden posts that allow one to traverse the bog without getting wet. Beneath the monastery there are catacombs that provide access to a subterranean river from which kobold slaves extract platinum ore. The abbot is a man named Thost whose skin is dyed aubergine.

Thost, Cleric Lvl 8: HP 31; AC 1 [18]; Save 8 (6 vs. paralysis and poison); CL/XP 9/1100; Special: Banish undead, spells (2/2/2/2/2). Platemail, shield, mace, throwing hammer, holy symbol.

0503.

A pass through the Aderumdoc Mountains here holds a weird town – a holdover from the days before the Sea Lords came to the Pirate Coast and the land was still occupied by small bands of exiles from the south. Nicknamed "Helltown" by the Sea Lords, they avoid it, for it is a wicked place.

Helltown is occupied by about 50 southmen and their servants and slaves, which increase the total population to 300. The town stands astride a swift stream of white water that tumbles into the lowlands below. It consists of numerous buildings constructed from dark gray stone. The buildings are square and uninspired and many have black poles at the corners hung with multi-colored streamers. These buildings are divided by wide boulevards clad in reddish tile. The intersections contain fire pits tended by slaves and kept burning all day and night with weird oils and wood gathered from the highlands and bodies of spent slaves and prisoners. The land around Helltown is planted with hedges of blackberries, fields of mandragora root and gardens of ritual herbs. These gardens are tended by slaves taken from the surrounding country and overseen by hobgoblins armed with staves and daggers.

Some of the buildings are taller than others and occupied by the olive skinned people who dominated the coast after the fall of the stone giants. These towers consist of a subterranean slave pit/dungeon, a work chamber, a room for summoning demons, a library and laboratory and, at the top, the living quarters of the tower's owner, invariably a magic-user of level 4th to 7th. These magic-users have servants that include goblins in black waistcoats and powdered wigs, imps, homunculi and men and women in ornate chains. Each of these magic-users has a unique patron demon from whom they draw their power, and they are locked in unending machinations against one another.

A deep depression in the middle of the town is filled with spongy, black ground and surrounded by a number of obsidian pylons carved with demonic faces. Speaking the correct words causes these faces to spew forth gases that alter emotions, cause hallucinations and madness.

0507.

There is a large structure here, a mound first constructed by the ancient stone giants and then fortified with stone by the dwarves, who used it as a temple. The dwarves constructed a shaft about 100 feet deep to hold their cubical idol of Mother Rock at the bottom. This idol still exists, but the mound is now used by a college of druids, who have sealed the holy shaft with a bronze grate. The druids are stocky men and women with olive skin and platinum blond hair. They wear white robes over leather armor and carry long, curved swords. The druids resent the arrival of the Sea Lords and hate the damage the humanoid tribes do the woods. In revenge, they are growing a crop of mandragoras that they intend to turn into ogre-sized brutes. With these creatures they will drive the humanoids and Sea Lords from the region.

Mandragora: HD 1; AC 3 [16]; Atk 2 tentacles (1d4); Move 12 (B9); Save 17; CL/XP 3/60; Special: Constrict, light blindness, resistance to fire (50%), magic resistance (10%)

Druid: HD 4; AC 9 [10]; Atk 1 (1d6 or weapon or spell); Move 12; Save 13; CL/XP 6/400; Special: Shape change, cast spells as 6th level druid.

0514.

A lodge of sod and stone rests upon a hill surrounded by beeches that buzz with hornets. A small chimney in the lodge releases a thin wisp of smoke. The lodge is the dwelling of three deer women, sisters as ancient as the Pirate Coast who keep its lore and sing its tales. They are willing to share their stories with those who have stories to give in return. Their only treasure is a collection of ten large spears of white oak with heads of silver.

Deer Women: HD 2; AC 5 [14]; Atk 1 touch (save or sleep); Move 18; Save 16 (14 vs. magic); CL/XP 3/60; Special: Spells (charm person, irresistible dance).

0519.

On a headland jutting into a placid river there is a small structure of white stones – an artful pile more than an actual structure. Inside the structure there dwells a pitiable creature, a massive white worm with the eyes of an elf. The worm cannot speak, but it understands all languages and can imbue any person with any magic-user spell, provided they bring it a pound of grave dirt from a freshly buried maiden.

0522.

There is a ceremonial mound here dedicated to the gods from beyond the stars. The mound is 30 feet tall, 40 feet wide and 90 feet long. Atop the mound there is traced out the form of what appears to be a salamander outlined in chalk and white stones. Any use of magic-user spells atop the mound causes the entire object to shift into the ethereal plane, dropping anyone on the mound 60 feet into a freezing subterranean lake. The fall is surprisingly slow, as though the molecules of earth only hesitantly leave the material plane. The fall inflicts only 2d6 points of damage.

The shores of this lake, which is about 500 feet in diameter, is populated by weird men and women with pallid skin and matted hair decorated with phosphorescent fungus picked from the cave walls. The people are emotionless and almost zombie-like, and live off of the electric eels and small shellfish in the shallow waters. All of these people are sorcerers, invoking the names of their alien gods to powerful effect, and risking (5% chance) being consumed by the alien energies each time they do so.

Alien God Invoked	Effect
Aulabotepha	*Confusion*, for Aulabotepha is the god of falsehood who takes the form of a white ant with human eyes
Gnothor	*Animate dead*, for Gnothor is the god of death who takes the form of a hairless rodent with lemon-yellow skin and eyes of deepest blue
Iskehot	*Baleful curse*, for Iskehot is the terrible god of fate who takes the form of a black cat-thing wreathed in moaning souls
Krlh	*Shield*, for Krlh is the goddess of war, who takes the form of a pseudo-female with six arms, eight legs and twelve heads with serpent tongues and obsidian alicorns jutting from their skulls
M'harsao	*Lightning bolt*, for M'harsao is the god of eels who takes the form of a monstrous eel
Yudegostho	*Lower water*, for Yudegostho is the god of the lake who takes the form of a great octopus with tentacles tipped with human faces that contort and scream

0529.

An ancient abandoned prison stands here, dominating the landscape. The prison was constructed by the stone giants, and thus sized for giants. It is constructed of gray stone and has a single entrance blocked by two thick portcullises of steel. The prison consists of a tall, round building of four stories (20-ft tall each) lined with cages. There is a central guard tower in the middle of this larger tower and the floor of the large tower is actually a treadmill, meant to work the energy out of prisoners. The prison is now roamed by a few random jellies and giant rats. The only sentient inhabitant is the spectre of a stone giant murderer named Verc. Turning the treadmill requires 36 people, twelve horses or six oxen. It does nothing useful.

Verc: HD 7; AC 2 [17]; Atk 1 spectral touch (1d8 + level drain); Move 15 (Fly 30); Save 9; CL/XP 9/1100; Special: Drain 2 levels with hit, immune to non-magical weapons.

0601.

The Aderumdoc Mountains here are home to a heavily fortified monastery of uneven copper-colored stones. The monastery is constructed atop a mountain and can only be reached by climbing sheer, 100-ft cliffs. Few ever make it to the summit. The monastery has no doors and open windows, allowing the elements free access to all but the innermost sanctum of the temple, where sits the abbess, Zumba the Prime, in quiet meditation. The brothers of the monastery call themselves Zarathustrans, and believe they have moved beyond humanity. They are emotionless and logical, spending their days in drug-induced meditation and the purging themselves of the fumes of the black lotus through exercise and martial training.

The monks number 10 postulants (1st level monks) and three brothers (3rd level monks). The abbot is Zumba the Prime, a gaunt man with a high forehead and shaved head. The monks keep a treasure of 2,000 sp, 1,885 gp and three gemstones – obsidian (200 gp) and two smoky quartz (10 gp).

Zumba the Prime, Monk Lvl 11: HP 32; AC 0 [19]; Save 5; CL/XP 10/1400; Special: Weaponless damage (3d8+1), two attacks per round, weapon damage +5, move 22, deadly strike (75% stun, 25% kill), only surprised on 1 in 6, deflect missiles, climb walls 95%, delicate tasks 80%, hear sounds 6 in 6, hide in shadows 85%, move silently 90%, open locks 85%, slow fall any distance, speak with animals, mastery of silence, mastery of mind, mastery of body, mastery of self, oneness with self. Spiked gauntlets (1d4 damage), brass medallion worth 155 gp.

Zarathustran Brother, Monk Lvl 3: HP 8; AC 7 [12]; Save 13; CL/XP 2/30; Special: Weaponless damage (1d6), weapon damage +1, move 14, deadly strike (75% stun, 25% kill), only surprised on 1 in 6, deflect missiles, climb walls 87%, delicate tasks 25%, hear sounds 4 in 6, hide in shadows 20%, move silently 30%, open locks 20%. Spiked gauntlets (1d4 damage).

Zarathustran Postulant, Monk Lvl 1: HP 3; AC 9 [10]; Save 15; CL/XP B/10; Special: Weaponless damage (1d4), move 12, deadly strike (75% stun, 25% kill), only surprised on 1 in 6, deflect missiles, climb walls 85%, delicate tasks 15%, hear sounds 3 in 6, hide in shadows 10%, move silently 20%, open locks 10%. Spiked gauntlets (1d4).

0605.

There is an old trail here, the soil pounded into stone by the action of dwarf mallets, feet and their iron-shod ponies over the centuries. The trail is often quite narrow, and every few miles there is a tree with a secret entrance into a root cellar holding long, purple tubers that taste of cinnamon, casks of pale ale and mead and various supplies like rope, leather sacks and torches.

The trail finally pierces a narrow gap in the Aderumdoc Mountains. The cliffs to either side of the trail stand 40 feet tall, and are in fact watch towers hollowed out by the dwarves and pierced with arrow slits so cleverly hidden as to be almost invisible to non-dwarves. The watch towers are usually manned by 1d6+4 dwarves each armed with crossbows, hand axes and long spears. The watch towers can only be entered from tunnels that run beneath the trail, tunnels that lead to the dwarf fortress-butte of Zimony located to the west of the area depicted on the enclosed map.

0610.

These wooded hills are haunted by a strange man, maybe a spirit of the woods, who appears as an aged man, long and lank with a wondrous beard and mustache of silver and chestnut and buck teeth through which he whistles a merry tune. The man wears a slouch hat of burled ivory felt and a gray suit of clothes – cloak, trousers and buttoned tunic. Wandering monster encounters in this hex are always with this man, who seems to act towards a goal that is incomprehensible to others. He is usually friendly to helpless strangers, but randomly guides them back towards civilization or deeper into the mysterious woods. He is an expert riddler and a stern task master who can, with a month of intensive training, put a person onto the path of the druid or ranger with ease (i.e. can train people to be 1st level rangers or druids and bestows them a +10% bonus to earned experience points for one level). He also knows everything there is to know about the wooded hills (locations, personalities, etc.), but shares his knowledge only with folk he has taken a liking to.

Bearded Stranger: HD 12 (70 hp); AC 6 [13]; Atk 1 hickory staff (1d6 or weapon or spell); Move 15; Save 3; CL/XP 14/2600; Special: Shape change, command plants and animals, raise or quell storms and winds, foretell the future in rhyme, cast fire, water, air and earth spells (cleric, druid or magic-user) each once per day as a 12th level caster.

0631.

Nin are furry humanoids about 4 feet in height with sleek, dark brown fur. Their heads resemble those of seals or otters, but they have four beady, black eyes. Nins are extremely fast, and each round can make two attacks and take two moves. Nin warriors rarely wear armor. They carry long daggers and slings. A band of 30 of the creatures dwells here in woven huts sitting crane style on posts driven into the mud.

The nin are famous as thieves and shysters, but are well regarded for the mystic beers they brew from the bark of swamp trees. These beers can either return 1d4 hit points to injured people or grant visions about the future. The band is led by an aged female called Pith, who wears a patchwork cloak of brilliant blue hues and carries a crooked walking stick.

Nin: HD 1d6; AC 3 [16]; Atk 1 bite (1d4) and 1 weapon (1d4); Move 24; Save 17; CL/XP 1/15; Special: Extra attack, mystic beer, surprise (3 in 6).

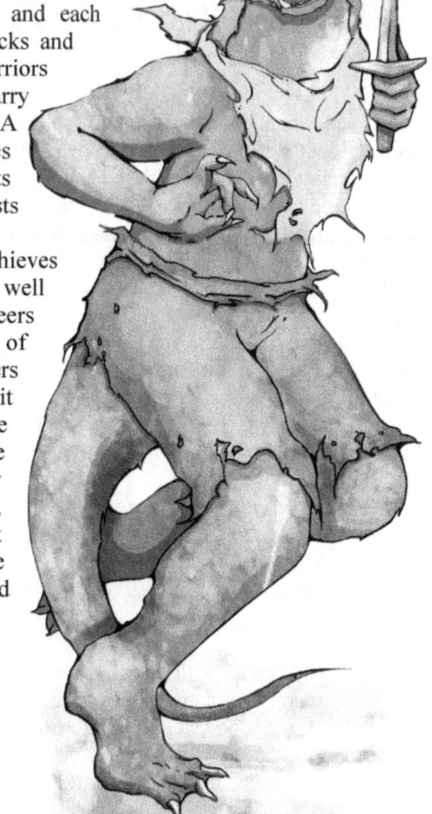

0711.

A snoot of ten orcs with pointed helms, cleaver-like axes and crossbows is operating here as highwaymen, relieving passing merchants of their valuables and then sending them along (except for the few who were chosen to be dinner). The orcs have amassed a small treasure consisting of a brass compass, 3,400 cp and a bill of sale that guarantees the delivery of 2,000 gp worth of topaz from the dwarves of the Granite Teeth tribe [0801].

0715.

Fat Sanan is a fur trader living in a small trading post in the woods. The post consists of a blockhouse surrounded by a wooden stockade with walls about 15 feet tall. The stockade encompasses about one acre of land. Sanan is an ex-pirate and a working smuggler, as well as a card cheat and a back stabber. He is married to Avena, an elf woman with a crooked smile. As pretty as she is, in that elusive, almost unnerving elf way, Avena is as untrustworthy as any creature that has ever lived. Fat Sanan has two locked chests containing about 500 gp worth of pelts and furs and a store full of ordinary supplies. His most prized possession in buried in the yard underneath a barren of rainwater. This is an oddly shaped stone that was chipped from the first human temple in the world. It is kept in a small clay jar filled with salt and sealed with straw and wax. In the hands of a cleric, the stone increases their level in terms of spell casting and turning undead by three.

Fat Simon, Thief Lvl 6: HP 17; AC 7 [12]; Save 11 (9 vs. devices); CL/XP 5/240; Special: Back stab x3, climb walls 90%, delicate tasks 35%, hear sounds 4 in 6, hide in shadows 30%, move silently 40%, open locks 30%, read languages, read magic writings. Leather, daggers (2), garrote, short sword, short bow, thieves' tools.

Avena, Elf Thief Lvl 4: HP 7; AC 7 [12]; Save 12 (10 vs. devices); CL/XP 3/60; Special: Darkvision 60 ft., find secret door on 4 in 6, immune to paralysis from ghouls , back stab x2, climb walls 88%, delicate tasks 30%, hear sounds 4 in 6, hide in shadows 25%, move silently 35%, open locks 25%, read languages, read magic writings. Leather armor, short sword, dagger, darts (5), thieves' tools.

0721.

On a windswept plain there stands a statue of a hawk-nosed man with a sneering mouth. The statue is carved from basalt and looks unfinished. It has been painted in places with red and white paint, and around the base there are dried gibbets of meat and humanoid organs left as offerings. The statue has four drums at his feet, carved from the stone but having skins of dragonhide and thus playable as actual drums. The drums contain the Four Terrible Winds of the Black God – ancient spirits that can be released only by playing the four drums in unison for four days and nights. Requires four successive constitution checks at cumulative daily penalties of -2 (i.e. -2 on the first day, -4 the second, etc.)

The drumming attracts the local humanoids, which flock to the statue to watch the spirits be unleashed. Bands of goblins (1d30+30), orcs (1d20+25) and hobgoblins (1d20+15) all come to the ritual, taking 1d4 days each to make it there.

Once released, the spirits emerge from the drums, which tear open. Each spirit looks like an animal and rushes from the drum like a wind. The Wolf Wind streaks south, blighting crops and withering trees. The Buzzard Wind streaks to the east, rousing the people to war. The Rat Wind streaks north, stirring men and women to kill their neighbors and making murderers of them. The final wind is the White Rabbit Wind, who streaks to the west and carries with it joy, hope and prosperity.

Each spirit travels many miles and then roosts in a single hex. The effects of the winds persist until all four of the spirits are chained in iron and carried back to the statue and sealed in their drums with dragon hides prepared by a druid of at least 9th level. If destroyed, a spirit simply reappears one week later.

Wolf Wind: HD 15; AC 5 [14]; Atk 1 bite (2d6+1); Move 18; Save 3; CL/XP 16/3200; Special: Breathe frost (1/turn), double damage to Lawfuls,+1 or better weapon to hit, magic resistance (45%), immune to cold and fire.

Buzzard Wind: HD 12; AC 6 [13]; Atk 2 claws (2d8), 1 bite (2d6+1); Move 3 (F20); Save 3; CL/XP 13/2300; Special: Double damage to Lawfuls, +1 or better weapon to hit, magic resistance (30%), immune to cold and fire.

Rat Wind: HD 9; AC 6 [13]; Atk 2 claws (1d6), 1 bite (2d6); Move 12; Save 7; CL/XP 9/1100; Special: Cause disease (mummy rot) with bite , double damage to Lawfuls, +1 or better weapon to hit, magic resistance (15%), immune to cold and fire.

White Rabbit Wind: HD 9; AC 6 [13]; Atk 2 claws (1d6), 1 bite (2d6); Move 12; Save 7; CL/XP 9/1100; Special: Double damage to Chaotics, +1 or better weapon to hit, magic resistance (15%), immune to cold and fire.

0727.

In a clearing there is a wide oak stump. Sitting on the stump there is a smallish Albian with a creased face and lank auburn hair. The man is eating an apple and smoking a plain, wooden pipe. He is intently studying a large, leather-bound book in which he has drawn, in colored inks, the human anatomy. While the man scratches his head, a female elf in the garb of a woodsman and with a terrible bite wound on her side winces in pain on the ground beneath his feet. Her wound is bandaged, and as she moans in pain the man clicks his tongue and tells her to be patient, for the differences in human and elf anatomy could prove fatal if he does not take care.

Inber, Leech Lvl 6: HP 16; AC 7 [12]; Save 0 (+1 vs. disease and poison); CL/XP 6/400; Special: Leechcraft (comrades have x2 normal healing and +1 to save vs. poison and disease), chirurgery (as turn undead, save against number of dice of healing he wants to apply to patient; success means the healing occurs, failure means he inflicts 1d6 damage), surgeon's precision (-3 to hit for double damage vs. humans, elves and orcs); Special: Leather armor, daggers (3) ,darts (10), leechs' tools, bandages, unguents and tonics, leechbook.

Thrista, Elf Fighter/Magic-User Lvl 4: HP 11; AC 9 [10]; Save 11; CL/XP 4/120, Special: Darkvision 60 ft., find secret door on 4 in 6, immune to paralysis from ghouls, multiple attacks, parry, spells (3/2). Longsword, hand axe, darts (8), long bow.

0730.

An ancient dome first constructed by the stone giants stands near a stream on a swampy lowland. The dome was an arena of sorts of the stone giants, where gladiatorial combat was conducted between rivals in love and between athletes and cave bears. The dome can be entered via two gates – one on the south and one on the north of the structure. The gates are barred by portcullises (*wizard locked*). These gates open onto tunnels that lead to the arena floor and also branch off into a tunnel that runs the perimeter. This perimeter tunnel allows access to the bleachers via staircases and to the tunnels underneath the arena that are now flooded.

The arena is now inhabited by a crooked old lich called Humladil the Horrid, a member of the ancient stocky race that once dwelled in the highlands in caves far from the stone giants. Humladil is skeletal, but has a droopy gray mustache and a cracked skull. He keeps a pack of mountain lions as guardians, allowing them to hunt in the hex but summoning them back each night to patrol the arena. The flooded tunnels contain a secret chamber wherein is hidden the lich's phylactery, a large diamond worth 7,500 gp.

The lich's treasure consists of 1,100 gp, a whalebone quill (100 gp), an alabaster statuette of a pretty maid preparing for a bath (50 gp), a tarnished golden lamp (10 gp), a heavy copper torc intended for a stone giant (30 gp), a white pine short bow and a grimoire with a cover of dark aqua-colored leather. The lich keeps it stacked in a dozen small caches in the walls, each one trapped with a scything blade designed to take off a person's hand. Those who reach into a cache for the coins must pass a saving throw or suffer 1d6 points of damage. Those who fail the saving throw by more than 10 points lose their hand.

Humladil's grimoire contains the following spells: 1st - *Charm person, magic missile, read languages, shield*; 2nd – *Darkness, invisibility, knock, strength*; 3rd – *Dispel magic, haste, hold person, monster summoning I, slow*; 4th – *Confusion, dimension door, polymorph self*; 5th – *Cloudkill, feeblemind, teleport, wall of stone*; 6th – *Monster summoning VI.*

Humladil the Lich: HD 12 (52 hp); AC 0 [19]; Atk 1 hand (1d10 + automatic paralysis); Move 6; Save 3; CL/XP 15/2900; Special: Appearance causes paralytic fear, touch causes automatic paralysis, spells as 12th level magic-user..

Mountain Lion: HD 5; AC 6 [13]; Atk 2 claws (1d4), 1 bite (1d8); Move 12; Save 12; CL/XP 5/240; Special: None.

0801.

This hex is the range of a sycorex (a prehistoric flying lizard just slightly smaller than a black dragon) the local dwarves call Andlat. The beast perches atop the tall, fang-like mountains of granite that rise in this hex, their lower slopes being covered with scrub oak, dandelions, bloodroot and jack-in-the-pulpit. The dwarves of the mountains dwell in deep caves in clans of 1d6 x 5 individuals. The dwarves of the Granite Teeth tribe are known to be extremely clannish and wary of outsiders. They are often called "bluddwergs" by other dwarves because of their almost uniformly red clothing, dyed in the sap of the bloodroot. The dwarves hunt the small mammals and birds in the area, dig up grubs and roots and mine their caves for topaz, which they trade via the subterranean trade routes to other dwarves for supplies. They brew dandelion wine, dandelion coffee and root beer, all of which find a ready market among the other dwarves of the mountains and the Sea Lords of the coast. The women of the dwarf clans are well versed in natural magic and the art of medicinal herbs, having the ability to cast spells as druids of 1st to 3rd level. Encounters in this hex are always with either the sycorex (75%) or the dwarves (25%). When out in the open, the dwarves are armed with axes or picks and carry short bows. Their arrows are dipped in bloodroot sap and cause burning pain (-1 to AC and to hit) unless a victim saves vs. poison.

Sycorex: HD 5 (22 hp); AC 2 [17]; Atk 2 claws (1d4), 1 bite (2d8); Move 9 (Fly 24); Save 12; CL/XP 7/600; Special: Shriek

0804.

These grassy highlands are now only inhabited by vicious rock weasels (encountered in groups of 1d3 on a roll of 1-3 on 1d6) and the prairie cockatrice (encountered alone on a roll of 1 on 1d6). The rock weasels, immune to the cockatrice's bite, prey on the creatures, keeping their population relatively low. About 20 years ago the villagers who grazed sturdy goats on the grass had to flee when petroleum began bubbling up to the surface and forming slicks in the low areas of the hex. A few ruined villages dot the hex – collections of a few toppled huts and wooden pens for the livestock.

Giant Rock Weasel: HD 4; AC 2 [17]; Atk 1 bite (2d6); Move 9; Save 13; CL/XP 5/240; Special: Stone breath.

0808.

At the crossroads of two well-worn trails there is an old roadhouse built of red bricks. The inn measures two stories tall, with thick windows of yellowish glass and a front door painted a cheery blue. The inn is surrounded by shaggy clumps of lavender and there are beehives behind the building buzzing with activity (and frequently drawing the attention of the local werebears – there is 1 in 12 chance per visit that the hives are under attack).

The roadhouse is owned by Adwen, a lovely woman with a reputation for her hospitality and her skill in medicine. Adwen has a staff of five living in the roadhouse with her, all ex-warriors that have retired to the roadhouse. Their mistress is a foxwere that has the warriors (3rd level fighters) under her control. While she is not especially sinister, she has sent her men into the wilderness to play the role of highwaymen when she takes a shine to something owned by one of her guests. Otherwise, she plays the perfect hostess – engaging, charming and keeping an excellent table. In her cellar she has casks of ale, mead and cider, all manner of dried herbs, sides of venison taken by her warriors in the woods.

In a pretty, locked cabinet she keeps vials and jars of honey infused with medicinal properties. When drizzled on bread and consumed, the honey can cure up to 1d4 points of damage or has a 35% chance to cure normal diseases and a 15% chance to cure mummy rot. When mixed with water and applied to the eyes, it has a 65% chance to cure blindness. Adwen happily sells her preparations at the price of 50 gp per jar. She keeps 1d4+1 jars in her cabinet. She has a treasure of 400 sp and 165 gp.

Foxwere: HD 3 (14 hp); AC 3 [16]; Atk 1 bite (1d4) or weapon (1d6); Move 15; Save 14; CL/XP 5/240; Special: Charm gaze, only harmed by silver weapons, surprise (2 in 6).

0812.

A pack of seven worgs has made a lair for itself in a cave beneath a large oak tree. The worgs are mercenaries, sometimes working with the local goblins to raid and plunder. The worgs hunt in this hex and the hexes surrounding it. In this hex, encounters with them occur on a roll of 1-4 on 1d6. In the surrounding hexes, encounters occur normally.

Worg: HD 4; AC 6 [13]; Atk 1 bite (1d6+1); Move 18; Save 13; CL/XP 4/120; Special: None.)

0818.

The river here is crossed by a stone bridge with a wooden canopy. The entrances on either end are carved with images of squirrels, acorns and owls, and sprigs of mistletoe hang over the entrances. The banks of the river are overhung with moody, swaying trees and the listless river seems to claw at its banks and hiss at the approach of people. The bridge is rarely crossed, for it is haunted by the phantom of a child with cruel eyes and wrapped in a long cloak.

The child was called Infre, and was the issue of a magic-user of questionable sanity and a demon. After poisoning several playmates, Infre was chased to the river and killed by an arrow in the back from a local hunter. Infre's body shriveled unnaturally and his bones were placed within the stonework of the bridge, was then under construction. His presence as a phantom has made the bridge unusable to most folk in the area, though some of the braver traders attempt crossings when there is a great deal of money at stake.

Phantoms are translucent spirits of creatures that died a particularly violent death. They have no attack form other than causing fear by their malevolent gaze, the fear striking any living creature within 30 feet of it that fails a saving throw. Affected creatures flee in terror for 1d6 rounds. A phantom is immune to all attack forms but can be destroyed through the casting of *dispel evil.*

0823.

These woodlands are haunted by creatures that look like tall, beautiful human beings wearing shaggy clothing made from pine boughs and carrying long-handled axes. The creatures are as tall as their surroundings – thus up to 100-feet tall around very tall trees and as small as blades of grass in meadows. The creatures, who call themselves the gallwaggu, are mischievous and often vengeful if they feel themselves mistreated. They don't appear to have lairs, simply sleeping where they take a fancy and dining on whatever creatures cross their paths, animal, human or otherwise.

Gallwaggu: HD 8 (1 hp/HD if tiny, 8 hp/HD if tall); AC 6 [13]; Atk 1 strike (1d4 + hp/HD); Move 12; Save varies; CL/XP varies; Special: Change height.

1002.

There is a village of leather tents here, located atop a craggy hill covered with hemlock. The village is inhabited by fifty shaggy men and their fifteen wives and thirty children. The women of the tribe are hairless and terribly thin. They wrap themselves in buckskin robes and huddle by the camp fire, whispering chants to curse their enemies. The men are rambunctious and crude, wielding clubs and stone axes. Their prey, human or animal, is skinned, the meat cut away and the fat rendered into bits of tallow that the men then chew upon during the day as a modern person might chew gum.

Shaggy Men: HD 3; AC 6 [13]; Atk 1 weapon (1d8+1); Move 12; Save 14; CL/XP 3/120; Special: Surprise on roll of 1-3 on 1d6.

1006.

Mother of pearl coats the interior of a winding cave that spirals downward into the ground. The spiral tunnel has many small branches burrowed into its sides. These burrows were dug by kobolds – many different broods that hate one another and compete for the meager supply of tourmalines in the granite and schist.

At the bottom of the spiral there is a large, empty throne room where once sat Florius the Kobold King before he angered those spirits that lurk beyond the veil. Florius is now a great mass of wriggling flesh that shifts and mutates before one's eyes. Five handmaidens surround the thing that was Florius. They wear green robes and alternately fan the creature with palm fronds and whip it with leather straps. The whipping is concentrated on pustules that appear on the skin. As these pustules burst, thoqqua fall onto the floor and rush to the walls, burrowing into and cocooning themselves – a month later, they emerge as fire phantoms. Three of these fire phantoms now guard the room and their father.

The throne room has four exits, each a broad staircase leading to a large cavern that howls with angry winds. Hidden in the ceiling of each passageway is a stone chest that can be lowered by pushing up on the "tile" it appears to be and then releasing four steel catches. Each of these chests contains 3d6 x 1,000 sp, 1d8 x 100 gp. The one in the passageway leading to [A] also holds a brass belt set with olivines (worth 210 gp).

Florius: HD 8 (40 hp); AC 3 [16]; Atk 2 claws (1d4); Move 9; Save 8; CL/XP 10/1400; Special: Corporeal instability (save or an amorphous mass and lose 1 point of Wisdom; new save every round, if wisdom becomes 0 the transformation is permanent), magic resistance (25%).

Hand Maiden: HD 2+1; AC 7 [12]; Atk 1 open hand slap (1d4); Move 12; Save 16; CL/XP 3/60; Special: Immune to charms and polymorph, ESP, psychic scream (save or confusion for 1d4 rounds).

Thoqqua: HD 3; AC 1 [18]; Atk 1 slam (1d6 + 2d6 fire); Move 12 (B9); Save 14; CL/XP 3/60; Special: Immune to fire, double damage from cold, things touched might burst into flames.

Fire Phantom: HD 6; AC 6 [13]; Atk 1 slam (1d4 + 1d6 fire); Move 6; Save 11; CL/XP 7/600; Special: Fire blast, immune to fire, immolation.

A – A band of adventurers are backed into a corner by two stone leopards. A third leopard lies on the ground, shattered into three large parts that still wriggle and kick. The party consists of three adventurers, the barbaric warrior Ingald, the elf Thorva and Osborn the halfling. Their magic-user has been torn in two and their cleric is lying in a pool of gore, barely clinging to life.

Ingald, Fighter Lvl 5: HP 25; AC 4 [15]; Save 10; CL/XP 5/240, Special: Multiple attacks, parry. Chainmail, battle axe, hand axe, dagger, javelins (5), short bow, 205 gp.

Thorva, Elf Fighter/Magic-User Lvl 4: HP 9; AC 9 [10]; Save 11; CL/XP 5/240, Special: Darkvision 60 ft., find secret door on 4 in 6, immune to paralysis from ghouls, multiple attacks, parry, spells (3/2). Longsword, dagger, long bow, 90 cp, 50 sp, 154 gp.

Osborn, Halfling Fighter Lvl 4: HP 27; AC 6 [13]; Save 11 (7 vs. magic); CL/XP 4/120, Special: Multiple attacks, parry, +1 to hit with missile weapons. Leather armor, shield, light mace, dagger, sling, 8 gp, glass urn worth 165 gp and a terracotta pitcher worth 3 gp.

Stone Leopard: HD 4; AC 3 [16]; Atk 1 slam (1d8); Move 12; Save 13; CL/XP 6/400; Special: Resistance to edged and piercing weapons (50%), immune to magic.

B – This cavern serves as the lair of eleven zoraks, brutish beetle men with coal black carapaces and burning red eyes. Each zorak has four arms, two with large, human hands and the other two with scythe-like blades. The creatures sit around a pit of burning coals. They make a living waylaying adventurers heading into the depths and have collected 5,195 sp, two pearls (worth 35 gp each) and four casks of olive oil (100 lb each, worth 150 gp each) in treasure. They seek curious round lodestones scattered throughout the dungeon that, when brought together, form a metallic creature that moves and behaves like an ooze. This creature dwells in the bottom of the coal pit.

Zorak: HD 4+1; AC 1 [18]; Atk 2 claw (1d4) and 2 blades (1d8); Move 9 (C9); Save 13; CL/XP 9/1100; Special: Immune to fire, victims of blade attack must save or be disarmed.

Lodestone Ooze: HD 10; AC 1 [18]; Atk 1 slam (1d6) or surge; Move 9; Save 5; CL/XP 12/2000; Special: Surge (move at double speed, opponents must save or be buried for 2d6 damage), iron weapons adhere to the creature with a successful hit, iron weapons within 20 feet fly from people's hands (open doors roll to resist) to the creature, weapon resistance (50%).

C – The walls of this chamber are riddled with tubes that appear to be composed of living, pink tissue. These wriggling tubes appear in bunches, and stick about 6 inches to one foot out of the walls, but they can extend up to 15 feet, attacking as a 2 HD creature. Any creature hit by one of the tubes begins to be cloned in a deeper chamber. The clone is fully formed in 6 rounds if the link is not broken before then, gaining a sixth of the original's abilities and levels each round. After 6 rounds, the clone is fully formed and the original must pass a saving throw or have their soul and being transferred into it, their own body being inhabited by a demonic spirit. The tubes can be severed with 6 points of damage, but any other tube attached can continue the cloning process. The room contains twenty of the tubes. The clones are, of course, born naked and weaponless, making ones transference into a clone a dangerous prospect.

D – This chamber is coated with super-slick grease that drizzles from the ceiling. Anyone walking in the room must pass a dexterity check each round to avoid falling for 1 point of damage and potentially sliding through the room in a random direction. The grease is impossible to wash off, but it does wear off in one week. Until then, it attracts wandering monsters, which appear on a roll of 1-2 on 1d6 made each hour.

1010.

There is a large, pyramidal structure of limestone constructed here, now partially obscured by tall pines. The pyramid is taller than it is wide and was constructed by the ancient stone giants as a granary. The large doors of the pyramid are constructed of stone and blend with the walls of the pyramid and would be difficult to find if there wasn't a ramp leading up to it. Inside the pyramid, which has not been visited for some time, there is about five tons of grain, much of it fermented and some of it infested with ergot fungi. The stone giants ferment the grain on purpose, and they find ergot fungi a pleasant and mild hallucinogen, unlike the humans, for whom it is a much more powerful drug. Those eating the grain must save

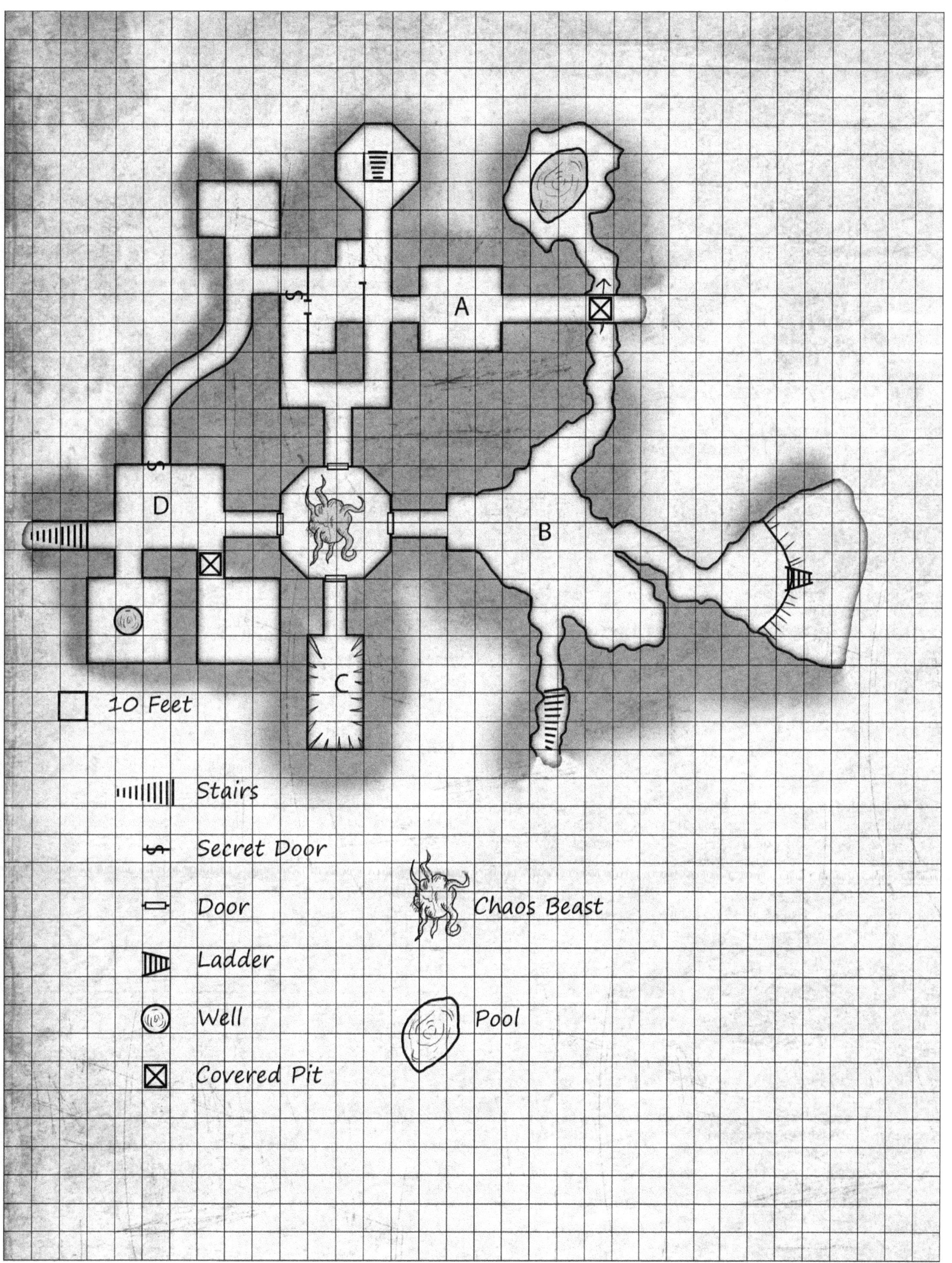

A
B
C
D
10 Feet
Stairs
Secret Door
Door
Ladder
Well
Covered Pit
Chaos Beast
Pool

each day or be struck with *insanity* (as the spell).

Opening the stone door causes the grain to rush out, potentially knocking people for a loop (save or suffer 2d6 damage). As the grain pours out, there is a 1 in 6 chance per round of 1d4 brain rats pouring out as well. They won't be happy about their little treasure trove being tampered with.

Brain Rat: HD 1; AC 5 [14]; Atk 1 bite (1d2); Move 9 (C9); Save 17; CL/XP 3/60; Special: Surprise on 1-3 on 1d6, brain thrust 3/day (1d6 damage per point of victim's intelligence under 14), spells (ESP, confusion 1/day, feeblemind 1/day).

1015.

Fort Naomith was established here at the fork in Devil's River to guard against incursions into the more populated coast, and to act as a leaping board for colonizing the interior by the Sea Lords. The fort is small and composed of a wooden stockade with four timber towers and a central barracks. The towers are usually guarded, and scaffolding against the wall allows the archers within to lay down a field of fire against potential invaders. Just outside the walls there is a longhouse made of logs and sealed with moss and dried mud; a combination tavern and trading post popular with the troops and with adventurers heading into the interior. The surrounding countryside is populated by a few bands of prospectors and miners, for the land is rich in iron and silver. Ancient kobold mines already dot the area, and many are still inhabited by the vile little creatures. The fort is commanded by Dudoga, a scholarly warrior interested in botany appointed to his position by the lord mayor of Amistie [1615]. Dudoga is a portly man, analytical and self-effacing, with long, thick, blond hair and gray eyes. He commands ten light horsemen and ten longbowmen.

1025.

An angry river flows through this hex, interrupted with smooth, red stones and caressed by black willows. Angry is not just a descriptive term for the river rapids, but a fact, for the river is possessed by angry spirits of woodland creatures and fey killed without the killer asking for forgiveness. Anyone drinking from the river must pass a saving throw or become angry and vengeful themselves for an entire day. If that drinker has killed an animal or fey in the woodland without asking its forgiveness, the water burns their throat as a deadly poison.

1030.

Nestled among the crooked trees and shallow pools of the swamp is the smuggler's paradise, Rogues' Harbor. Rogues' Harbor is constructed around a deep pool that connects to the sea via a maze of deep channels that can be sailed by shallow draft boats like galleys. The necessary charts are made available to pirates of thoroughly suspect character who come across with a sizable donation to agents stationed in the major settlements of the region. The charts must be memorized over the course of one night and are then destroyed.

The village is populated by about 50 permanent residents, but the arrival of one or more crews can double the population. The settlement consists of a couple dozen timber buildings camouflaged with hanging moss and creeping vines. Among the population are rope-makers, coopers, a full service smithy, five taverns, two carpenters and an alchemist, Almar, who was forced to the quiet village in the middle of the night under hot pursuit by the local authorities from the nearby town of Slakethirst.

Almar, quite naturally, lives a bit apart from the others, but his concoctions and elixirs are highly valued by the pirates. Even more valued are his vat-grown women, beauties all with only minor flaws that are usually hidden when physical or ignored when mental. Almar's women, as they are called, can be found lounging on his portico, dipping their toes in the water and cooling themselves with feathered fans when not negotiating a deal with an amorous visitor.

There is no particular law in Rogues' Harbor, but entrance into the place assumes agreement to a binding truce made before an altar of Alamia, the sea demoness, who representative priestess, Wolda, is not to be trifled with.

Wolda, Cleric Lvl 7: HP 24; AC 3 [16]; Save 9 (7 vs. paralysis and poison); CL/XP 8/800; Special: Banish undead, spells (2/2/2/1/1). Chainmail, shield, mace, sling, holy symbol.

1114.

The trees in his hex contain a number of dreys (i.e. squirrel nests) belonging to giant killer squirrels. Each drey is a large conglomeration of sticks and twigs set high in the trees. The squirrels have a dim, cunning intelligence, and they are capable of coordinating their attacks, communicating with bits of shiny glass and metal high in the treetops. There is a 4 in 6 chance of being attacked while moving through the hex. Attacks are by scurries of 3d6 x 3 squirrels, and each nest holds 1d6 squirrels and their treasure.

Killer Squirrel: HD 1d4 hp; AC 7 [12]; Atk 1 bite (1d4); Move 9; Save 18; CL/XP B/10; Special: Surprise (3 in 6).

1117.

At a crossroads here there are four breaking wheels set up at each corner of the crossroads. The breaking wheels hold four dead bodies that are quite talkative if one gives them a draught of wine. The bodies can answer questions about the area (i.e. provide rumors).

1122.

Lilian of the Golden Locks, a delicate woman of noble mein and black moods dwells here in a compact fortress of reddish granite in a wooded valley that points to the sea. The valley is thick with sheep and has a cluster of small stone hovels around the walls. The courtyard of the castle is maze-like in its construction, and the donjon is equally confusing. The whole is neglected and overgrown with moss. A number of magical herbs spring up in the courtyard maze under the full moon – wolvesbane among them.

Lilian has known much death in her life. A knight cruel and puissant, she rode down many enemies when still she lived in the White Isles. She is a beautiful woman, with long hair, green eyes and marble skin. She often wears gowns of indigo silk with a surcote of green damask silk while holding court in her little castle.. Lilian now lives as a bitter exile, turned away by her noble family in the White Isles when she fell in love with an elf. The two fled to the Pirate Coast and constructed their fortress, but soon the elf grew tired of her and went on his merry way, leaving her to pine away in a strange land, a gaggle of peasants for her company.

1124.

A hunting party of twenty goblins has set out three barrels of ripe strawberries as bait for a giant slug. The goblins are hiding behind clumps of vegetation. They wear leather armor and carry military forks, light crossbows, and small sacks of salt that can be thrown as grenades. When characters enter the area, roll 1d6

Roll	Action
1	Goblins remain hidden – they may be stupid enough to hunt giant slugs, but not adventurers
2-3	The goblins are tired of waiting – they ambush the adventurers, surprising on a roll of 1-2 on 1d6
4-5	A giant slug is silently slinking towards the strawberries – it is about 50 yards away
6	The goblins are engaged in combat with the slug, which has already lost half its hit points

The goblins hail from the village in [0218].

Giant Slug: HD 12; AC 8[11]; Atk 1 bite (1d12) or acid squirt; Move 6; Save 3; CL/XP 13/2300; Special: Spit acid."Slug, Giant")

1219.

A small black castle stands beside a lazy stream atop a small promontory of smooth, black rock. Stairs have been cut into the rock and lead to a door of thick hepatizon bearing a crest of an axe head. The surrounding countryside is morose, but fertile, and hosts a farming village of picturesque peasants of the Sea Lord race. The women of the village are Rubinesque and lovely, with lips like candied apples and long hair worn in braids. The men are sleepy-eyed and quiet, with luxurious mustaches and stubby, stout pipes that send curls of smoke around their heads. The men of the village keep goats and sheep and farm potatoes, gourds, barley and wheat. They brew dark, bitter beers and distill powerful vodka, and seem to sample their wares more than they export them.

The folk of the village are notoriously closed mouthed about the lord of the land, a reclusive philosopher named Vaurok. Vaurok is a tall man with sparse, black hair and skin made pallid by long absences from the light of the sun. Tall and noble, Vaurok has intense eyes that suggest a deep passion that overwhelms his common sense. In one of the three towers of his castle he has a wizard's laboratory and a small library. Stairs from the laboratory lead down to his great hall, and a secret door on the stairs gives access to a second set of stairs that lead into the dungeons, where he keeps prisoner his most recent creation, a flesh golem he has nicknamed Stram, after his maternal uncle and mentor. Vaurok almost regrets making the golem, and has almost decided to destroy it. His servants are unaware of the monster, but can feel the anxiety of their master and know it has something to do with the laboratory.

Vaurock, Magic-User Lvl 9: HP 22; AC 9 [10]; Save 7 (5 vs. spells); CL/XP 9/1100; Special: Spells (4/3/3/2/1). Staff, dagger, darts (10), spellbook.

Flesh Golem: HD 10 (45hp); AC 9 [10]; Atk 2 fists (2d8); Move 8; Save 5; CL/XP 12/2000; Special: Healed by lightning, hit only by magic weapons, slowed by fire and cold, immune to most spells.

1231.

Tall, black cypresses cover this hex of swampland. The shallow water hides rich deposits of gold-bearing quartz as well as spiny dragonfish and a lost army of skeletal stone giants. Encounters occur on a roll of 1-3 on 1d6, with 75% of those encounters being with dragonfish and the others with the twelve giant skeletons that are still clad in their ceremonial bronze armor and wield massive bronze studded clubs. The quartz makes itself apparent in large, natural pylons that hide among the trees. Travelers have a 1 in 30 chance of discovering such a pylon, which contains about 3 tons of quartz and maybe 100 pounds of gold.

Giant Skeleton: HD 9; AC 8 [11]; Atk 1 weapon (3d6); Move 12; Save 6; CL/XP 9/1100; Special: None.

Dragonfish: HD 2; AC 3 [16]; Atk 1 bite (1d4); Move S9; Save 16; CL/XP 3/60; Special: Poison spines (save or 1d6 damage, might snap off), surprise (4 in 6).

1301.

An old mine of rose quartz – long since played out and abandoned – burrows deep into a craggy hillside here. The mine consists of diagonal passages and spiral ramps leading from one level to another. The three levels present are about 30 feet apart, the lowest level extending only about 30 feet and then ending in bare stone – at this point, the miners gave up on finding more quartz. This dead end is actually a door hidden by a thick weave of illusion. The door is made of stone encased in a cage of wrought iron and hung with a dozen unholy symbols forged from black iron.

Behind this door there are three chambers, set one after the other and each lower than the last. The first chamber is wide and long and decorated with the trappings of a sailing ship – an uncommon thing in this world, where most vessels are galleys. The roof is shored up by thick ribs of oak and barrels and casks sealed with wax, empty, are scattered about the room

along with coils of oiled rope and tattered and faded pennons of unknown countries from across the sea. At the end of this room there is a portal edged in cinnabar that gives off a weird hum as living creatures draw near. Should a person attempt to step through the portal, an awesome gust of wind arises, forcing them and everyone else to make an open doors check or be thrown back into the room. The wind dies back down as quickly as it arose, but it rises again whenever one attempts to step through the portal. Moreover, it awakens the two rope golems that guard the room.

Rope Golem: HD 5; AC 7 [12]; Atk 2 slams (2d6); Move 6; Save 12; CL/XP 6/400; Special: Strangulation (1d8 damage if both slams hit same victim), double damage from fire, immune to magic (rope trick does 1d6 damage).

The next chamber, should one manage to make it there, is much smaller than the last. This room is decorated as an alchemist's laboratory. It contains a workbench running down the middle covered with alembics, crucibles, beakers, vials and other alchemical sundries. One corner holds a metal box – an oven that holds a captive hearth elemental that provides heat without smoke. The south wall is given over to shelves hung from bronze chains. These shelves hold dried animal specimens, jars of dried and preserved herbs, leaves, berries and fruit, bat wings in oil, goose eggs in brine, glass marbles and prisms, bits of lead and other metals and wooden boxes holding vials of mercury and antimony. A large safe with a complex (-20%) lock holds alchemical products such as barium glowstones, quicklime, pitchblende, natron, lunar caustic, saltpeter, copperas and butter of antimony. All in all, it is an impressive hoard of goodies for any magic-user.

Hearthfire Elemental: HD 1; AC 4 [15]; Atk 1 slam (1 + burn); Move 0; Save 17; CL/XP 3/60; Special: Start fire, light, immune to fire.

The north, east and west walls are decorated with a fresco of three rainbow-hued serpents with knowing eyes and ready fangs. They seem to wriggle and shift out of the corner of one's eye, and are in fact illusory guardians – permanent phantasmal killers etched into the wall with enchanted pigments. Any attempt to molest the goods in the laboratory cause them to "attack" and forcing folks in the room to pass a saving throw. If they fail, they are struck dead. If they succeed, they take a mere 3d6 points of damage. These illusory paintings hide a wooden door on the west wall.

Behind the wooden door there is a staircase that descends about 10 feet into a long hall. The hall is undecorated – just bare rock with six pillars running down the center and a throne carved from the living rock. The throne is surrounded by several piles of books and scrolls. This pile of literature contain numerous esoteric tomes that should aid magic-users in researching and creating spells, as well as two complete spell books, a manual of rope golem construction (requires a mirror to read properly) and a journal containing maps of the coast that seem wildly inaccurate, referring to settlements that do not exist.

Spellbook I: 1st – Detect magic, hold portal, magic missile, protection from evil, shield; 2nd – Detect invisibility, ESP, invisibility, stinking cloud; 3rd – Clairaudience, dispel magic, fly, haste, lightning bolt, protection from normal missiles;

Spellbook II: 4th – Hallucinatory terrain, ice storm, wall of ice; 5th – Animal growth, conjuration of elementals, magic jar, passwall; 6th – Geas, move earth, repulsion; 7th – Phase door..

Sitting atop this throne is a haggard bag of bones, a skeletal figure ensconced in a cloth-of-gold robe (worth 120 gp) and a sleeveless robe of crimson damask silk (worth 60 gp). The skeleton's teeth are exceptionally worn and its fingers are decorated with gold and silver rings (worth 300 gp). The skeleton is motionless for many minutes when adventurers enter the room for many minutes before finally sitting tall and asking in a lisping voice in an ancient tongue, "Why do you seek out my domicile? What fools are these to disturb my thoughts?"

The lich calls itself Cumont and is fairly open to negotiation and conversation, although there remains a 1% chance per turn spent in its presence that it grows bored with the conversation and seeks to destroy its visitors out of sheer maleficence.

Cumont: HD 14; AC 0 [19]; Atk 1 hand (1d10 + automatic paralysis); Move 6; Save 3; CL/XP 17/3500; Special: Appearance causes paralytic fear, touch causes automatic paralysis, spells as 14th level magic-user.

Cumont's phylactery is a reliquary of black metal with reddish glass that looks like a lantern. It hangs in the tavern of Rogues' Harbor [1030].

1306.

The swamp here contains a moot of the local treants. The moot is nothing more than an old, mossy boulder that serves as a marker for the treants. The treants resemble sweetgum trees and willows, and their personalities are as damp as their homeland. The moot, when in session, attracts 1d4+6 treants. There is a 3% chance of a moot being in session when travelers are passing through. Otherwise, encounters with the treants in this hex occur on a roll of 1-2 on 1d6.

1309.

A flock of giant bald eagles lives in the tree tops here. The eagles guard an ancient relic of the past, a magical *+2 shield* that protects its holder from fire, lightning and cold, cutting damage from these attacks by half. The shield is a round disc shaped from adamant and bearing a smiling face in silver.

Giant Bald Eagle: HD 4; AC 7 [12]; Atk 2 talons (1d4), 1 bite (1d8); Move 3 (Fly 24); Save 13; CL/XP 4/120; Special: None.

1313.

A sprawling farm here supports a large brick manor that has been converted by a sisterhood of nuns into a school for wayward girls. The manor is protected by the seven nuns, all clerics (roll 1d4 for level) and sages, who also teach the girls in the seven liberal arts – arithmetic, geometry, astronomy, music theory, grammar, logic and rhetoric. The girls help on the farm as best they can in their shackles (they are wayward, after all, and discipline is paramount). The farm grows barley and rye and keeps seven dairy cows, all sentient and capable of speech and employed to lecture the girls on moral dilemmas. The cows are the unfortunate victims of a notorious magic-user who once plagued the coast, and whose bones now bleach in the sun.

The manor retains the fine decoration of its first lord, Carr, a pirate who donated the manor to assuage his guilty conscience. The nuns have turned one chamber into a library of basic texts and another into a sanctuary with an idol of Albia carved from marble.

One of the maidens interred, a flighty girl named Amri, has a beau named Virs. Virs is a pirate mate of some note, having sailed with Red Kris, and he is currently lurking on the margins of the farm, taking stock of the place and planning a daring rescue.

Virs: HD 3 (18 hp); AC 7 [12]; Atk 1 axe (1d8); Move 12; Save 14; CL/XP 3/60; Special: None.

1327.

The village of Cours is ripe for rebellion. With the death of its beloved Baron Willem and the ascension of his obnoxious son, Kord, taxes have been raised and new restrictions have been placed on the peasants. Kord relies on his company of men-at-arms to keep the peace. The village is set on a green plateau on which are grown wheat and hemp and raise dairy cows, producing a fine cheese. In the Veiled Queen Tavern, peasants whisper over their posset and pass hastily scrawled messages to travelers in green. The travelers are rangers from beyond the plateau who oppose Kord and would see him replaced in favor of their leader (and his cousin), a ranger named Cala.

Cala, Ranger Lvl 7: HP 35; AC 5 [14]; Save 8; CL/XP 8/800; Special: Tracking, alertness, +7 damage vs giants and goblin-types. Ring armor, shield, long sword, hand axe, dagger, longbow, darts (3).

Kord, Fighter Lvl 5: HP 17; AC 1 [18]; Save 10; CL/XP 5/240, Special: Multiple attacks, parry. Platemail, shield, axe, dagger, longbow.

1411.

Artor is a sinister wood carver dwelling in a log cabin here. A bitter man who never had a friend in the world (and never earned one), Artor long ago came into the possession of a magic set of chisels. The chisels were the result of a trade with a mysterious man of dark features and pleasant demeanor. Any statue the man carves in the image of another animates with a strange semblance of life. The animated statue then begins tracking his double, unerringly. Although the statue moves slowly, it is tireless. As it grows closer to its quarry, it drains the life and memories from the person, slowly taking on the appearance of a human being as its new levels outnumber its original hit dice. When it is ten miles away, it drains its first level. Each additional mile closer, it drains another level. It cannot drain the person's last level until it has killed them in single combat.

Statue: HD 3; AC 5 [14]; Atk 1 strike (1d6+1) or by weapon; Move 9; Save 14; CL/XP 5/240; Special: Level drain, weapon resistance (50%), magic resistance (15%), can be turned as a 7 HD undead.

1415.

A gang of 1d6+6 satyrs frolics in the woods here. They are lustful and chaotic, and during the day they hide in a long, shallow cave, feeding on snails and drinking dandelion wine from clay jugs. Hidden in a crevice is a collection of suggestive etchings worth 20 gp.

Satyr: HD 5; AC 5 [14]; Atk 1 weapon (1d8); Move 18; Save 12; CL/XP 6/400; Special: Magic resistance (50%), pipes, concealment.

1418.

The silk pavilion of Hakar Pasha, a traveler from the spice-bearing islands of the south, has been erected here. The pasha is a mechanical man, as are all the aristocrats of the Spice Islands, constructed by the original rulers to serve as factotums and impartial magistrates and eventually imprisoning the whole of the nobility due to their unerring sense of justice. Hakar Pasha has two comrades, an old salt called Yeer and a hairy berserk from the western lands called Gund. The three boon companions seek to challenge Vaurock [1219] for a bauble now in his possession that belongs to the Court of the Mechanical King.

Hakar Pasha is rather round automaton, embossed with decorative palms and stars and wearing a tall hat of silk that acts as a bag of holding and a bristling mustachio of brass wires. Yeer is short and squat, with a scarred face and a velvet eye patch. His mouth is always decorated with a long, clay pipe. Gund is a hairy man wearing a cloak of bearskin and carrying a spear and bolo (1d4 damage, opponents must pass a saving throw or be tripped; a tripped opponent has a 1 in 6 chance of being entangled).

Hakar Pasha: HD 6 (35 hp); AC 2 [17]; Atk 1 mace (1d6+2); Move 12; Save 11; CL/XP 7/600; Special: Immune to mind effects, disease and poison.

Yeer: HD 6 (40 hp); AC 7 [12]; Atk 2 fists (1d3+3) or 1 cutlass (1d6+3); Move 12; Save 11 (8 vs spells); CL/XP 6/400; Special: None.

Gund: HD 6 (42 hp); AC 8 [11]; Atk 1 spear (1d6+1) or bolo; Move 15; Save 11 (9 vs poison and disease); CL/XP 6/400; Special: Can go berserk in combat (+1 to hit and damage, immune to fear) for 6 rounds.

1422.

Missionaries of Albia, the White Goddess, have established a hospice here to minister to the sick. They provide succor to poor and distressed travelers and healing to people poor enough that they cannot afford clerical ministrations in the towns and villages. The hospice is a building of gray stone, two stories tall and surrounded by medicinal gardens themselves surrounded by a low, stone wall. The hospice quarters 20 low-level clerics (half of them 1st level, seven of them 2nd level and three 3rd level) under a knight commander named Gall. Gall is a kind man, humble and self-effacing, with long hair and black eyes.

Gall, Cleric Lvl 9: 35; AC 1 [18]; Save 7 (5 vs. paralysis and poison); CL/XP 10/1400; Special: Banish undead, spells (3/3/3/2/2). Platemail, shield, war hammer, throwing hammer, holy symbol, copper bracelet (85 gp).

1424.

Next to a stream there is a large boulder with a hand imprinted in it. A person with a similarly sized hand (30% chance for human female or any elf, 10% chance for human male) can place it in the print and cause the boulder to invert and become a portal into a subterranean faerie land. This land of ghost-lit caverns is beautiful but dangerous. It is ruled by faerie princes and queens who compete for pointless titles and honors, jousts on elven steeds, sprites, satyrs, stately nymphs who serve as emissaries to the courts, beautiful, tall elves in mail coats and helms with long swords and daggers and hooded priestesses with animal faces. The faerie land extends for hundreds of miles underground. The boulder entrance is protected by a mihstu bound by faerie magic.

Mihstu: HD 8 (34 hp); AC -3 [22]; Atk 4 tentacles (1d6); Move 9 (F9); Save 8; CL/XP 13/2300; Special: Engulf (1d2 constitution damage per round), +1 weapon to hit, immune to electricity, resistance to missile attacks (including magic missile, 50% miss chance), magic resistance (15%), susceptible to cold.

1502.

The 300 elves of the Two Hawks tribe make their lair here on a broad meadow of sweet grasses and bluebells. The meadow is bisected by a rushing river and surrounded by black walnuts and hickories. The elves live in pavilions of sheep skin dyed in bright colors stretched over hickory frames. Before each pavilion there is planted a hickory staff topped by a bronze emblem, the armorial of the family that owns the pavilion.

The elves of the Two Hawks tribe stand about 5-ft in height and have the ears of foxes. Their skin is russet in hue and their hair ranges from platinum blond to raven black. They wear woolen kilts of green and yellow and in time of war supplement this costume with long coats of shimmering mail, oval wooden shields painted with their family's emblem, and wide, round helms tied under their chins with strips of leather branded with glyphs of prayer.

The elves have no chieftains. Instead, they use the "big man" system of rule in which an elf proposes a course of action (let us hunt upon the eastern ridge or let us make war on the goblins today) and whoever agrees with them follows along. The Two Hawks elves value family ties, humor and gossip above all things, and pride themselves in the spells handed down within each family. They provide for themselves by hunting in the woodlands and fishing in the rivers and are especially skilled at weaving and crafting jewelry from silver and gold (their treasures are 1/4 normal coins, x2 normal gems and jewelry).

The fiercest elves in the tribe are three siblings, Hjalmanan, Derbelinus and Sezabeth. All three are mighty warriors and magic-users and the tribe heeds their counsel above almost all others. Hjalmanan is brash and bold and given to weaving colorful stories to the delight of his tribesmen. Derbelinus is more grave and stable than his brother. Sezabeth is the swiftest and brightest of the three, and it is she who most often leads the elves in battle against their foes.

The Two Hawks tribe keeps a treasure of 1,600 sp, 1,480 gp

Hjalmanan, Elf Fighter/Magic-User Lvl 5: HP 13; AC 9 [10]; Save 10; CL/XP 6/400, Special: Multiple attacks, parry, spells (4/2/1). Battle axe, hand axe, longbow, hepatizon pendent worth 55 gp.

Derbelinu, Elf Fighter/Magic-User Lvl 5: HP 13; AC 9 [10]; Save 10; CL/XP 6/400, Special: Multiple attacks, parry, spells (4/2/1). Battle axe, hand axe, longbow.

Sezabeth, Elf Fighter/Magic-User Lvl 5: HP 19; AC 9 [10]; Save 10; CL/XP 6/400, Special: Multiple attacks, parry, spells (4/2/1). Battle axe, hand axe, longbow.

1507.

Three exotic nymphs, heleionomai to be precise, dwell in a shallow pool here surrounded by cypress trees. The pool can confer the *protection from evil* power for 1 week on any who bath in it. The nymphs, Sabria, Melega and Hersuine, have dark brown skin and hair the color of moonlight on a quivering pool. They are quite lovely, but flighty and temperamental, setting their "pet", a giant snapping turtle, on those who approach the pool without bearing the torch of Olchies, the stone giant god of petty vengeances [1708].

Heleionomai: HD 3 (17, 13, 10 hp); AC 9 [10]; Atk none; Move 12; Save 14; CL/XP 5/240; Special: Sight causes blindness or death.

Giant Snapping Turtle: HD 8 (29 hp); AC 2 [17] shell, 5 [14] head/limbs; Atk 1 bite (4d6); Move 4 (Swim 9); Save 8; CL/XP 8/800; Special: None.

1510.

Folk tromping through the woods in this hex may come across a wide, well-beaten trail. There is a 2 in 6 chance that they will see the creatures that made the trail, a herd of sixteen mastodons, seven of which carry on their backs holy men in deep meditation. The holy men are aged and wrinkled, with golden-brown skin and burnished, coppery hair sticking out from under black, cylindrical caps. The men wear loose, white robes. They are druids who are never parted from their mastodon mount – bathing with them, meditating with them and sleeping on their backs. The men wear white robes and carry cudgels, leather pouches in which they store holly, mistletoe, acorns and other ritual items of the druids and silver coronets that they use to communicate with their mounts. Mastodon and druid share a close bond, and are willing to fight to the death to defend one another. In all, there are fifteen mastodons and six druids in the herd.

Mastodon: HD 12; AC 5 [14]; Atk 1 trunk (1d10), 2 gore (1d10+4), 2 trample (2d6+4); Move 12; Save 3; CL/XP 13/2300; Special: None.

Druid: HD 4; AC 9 [10]; Atk 1 (1d6 or weapon or spell); Move 12; Save 13; CL/XP 6/400; Special: Shape change, spell-casting as 6th level druid.

1518.

The coast here is harassed by a sisterhood of warrior nymphs, beauteous women with skin the color of sea foam, flowing golden locks and byrnies of shells. The nymphs wield long serrated spears, coming up from their kelp gardens in the shallows to raid the surrounding farms and passing ships for goods they cannot produce under the sea. There are fifty nymphs in the sisterhood, each one as beautiful and proud as the rest.

Warrior Nymph: HD 3+3; AC 6 [13]; Atk 1 spear (1d8); Move 12; Save 14; CL/XP 5/240; Special: Sight causes blindness or death.

1611.

A little goddess sits here in a marble shrine with a dramatic, conical roof supported on three marble pillars. Great bunches of lavender grow around the shrine and hum with the activity of bumblebees. One might easily mistake the little goddess for an idol, for her skin is like brass and her eyes like olivines. She is a short, curvaceous woman who the local humanoids know as Trise, the goddess of fortune and hard work. In this form she wears golden coin armor.

Trise is happy to give advice in exchange for a precious gift and an hour of fervent prayers, and she might cast a spells under the same conditions. If attacked, she transforms into a strange creature, about 8 feet long and shaped like a four-legged bee clad in marble-like chitin, with shadowy wings that give off an icy breeze. Clerics who swear themselves to her worship receive a coin plucked from her armor as a holy symbol. Clerics must return at the full moon (at least once every three moons) to pay a tithe and fast for three days while meditating at her feet or they lose their spellcasting ability and must undertake a quest in her name.

Trise, Goddess of Fortune: HD 6 (48 gp); AC 2 [17]; Atk 2 claws (1d6); Move 15 (F24); Save 11; CL/XP 12/2000; Special: Alternate form, cast spells as 15th level cleric and 7th level magic-user, turn undead as 15th level cleric, only harmed by +1 or better weapons, magic resistance (45%).

1613.

There is an old, abandoned mill located on a creek here. The stones of the mill are weathered and the area is overgrown, suggesting has been empty for at least a decade. Sitting on a felled tree rubbing his feet is a curious man in a long, black cap, Victorian cape, tweed waistcoat and breeches and leather hiking boots. The man, who will introduce himself as Mortimer, carries an oak walking stick with a silver head and a leather pouch.

If asked his business, Mortimer will explain that he is a traveler a long way from home who needs desperately to gain access to the mill, but is barred by a rather unpleasant "fellow" inside. Mortimer is, of course, a plane hopping magic-user from another of the myriad Earths. He came to this world to locate a rather important artifact that had long ago been stolen away and hidden. He believes it is located in the mill, but it is now guarded by a powerful entity called a vril-ya, a demon in angel's guise as it were.

The relic in question is a magical *spear +1/+3 vs demons* that can be used as a *staff of command*. It is hidden in the mill as the pole on which turn the millstones. Mortimer knows he is not powerful enough to challenge the vril-ya, and seeks aid in defeating it.

Vril-ya: HD 10; AC -1 [20]; Atk 1 psychic blast (2d6); Move 12; Save 5; CL/XP 12/2000; Special: Psychic blast (cone 30-ft long, 10-ft wide at base, 2d6 damage or save for half), spells (at will - cure light wounds, ESP, inflict light wounds, polymorph other; 1/day – finger of death), telepathy 1 mile range.

Mortimer, Magic-User Lvl 9: HP 22; AC 9 [10]; Save 7 (5 vs. spells); CL/XP 9/1100; Special: Spells (4/3/3/2/1). Dagger, darts (6), spellbook.

1615.

The town of Amistie lies here, nestled on a harbor created by the intersection of the Green River and a lively stream. Amistie is not as large as Hofn. It still fits, snugly, into a wooden palisade with three gates – called the Fruit Gate that opens to the broader valley where grains and vegetables are grown, the Fish Gate, through which are carried the fruits of the river and ocean, and the West Gate, through which pass explorers, trappers and adventurers headed into the hinterland.

Amistie is known for its rugged stone churches (it has three, despite its small size), its well-stocked apothecaries (the finest on the coast) and the many intrigues between its nobility. Amistie has more families of noble descent than the other Sea Lord towns on the coast, and they have seen fit to organize themselves as the Council of Primacy, electing from their own number a Lord Mayor. Each noble family maintains a bodyguard that doubles as the town's army in times of trial. Policing is carried out by hired agents. Shopkeeps and artisans employ guards to keep their property safe, and thief-takers (often thieves themselves) to capture wrong-doers.

Despite this somewhat haphazard approach to public safety, Amistie has a fairly normal level of crime and the citizens are known for their down-to-earth friendliness. Wealth in Amistie comes from the pirate fleet of Ydence Longshanks and from the fine horses raised on the plantations that fill the quiet valley.

The current Lord Mayor is Heald Perch, a swaggering peacock with a minor talent at magic. Heald comes from a long line of noble blood but looks something like a gravedigger, having a buzzard-like face and pasty skin. He is the tallest man in Amistie (which is saying something given the height of most Sea Lords), with grey eyes and lank, black hair. His chief rival is one Thela Kenth, a spendthrift master goldsmith who excels at public oratory and who has paid off the lower class to support her campaign to break the power of the nobility. The nobles hate her, of course, and the artisans and merchants regard her with fear. Thela does not lack for enemies. She can usually be found "holding court" in the Blue House, a tavern near the docks.

Heald Perch, Magic-User Lvl 5: HP 8; AC 9 [10]; Save 11 (9 vs. spells); CL/XP 4/120; Special: Spells (4/2/1). Daggers (4), darts (10), vial of poison, spellbook.

1620.

The seaside plays host to the largest Albian temple in Namera. The building is about the size of a cathedral, and heavily fortified. Within the temple there is a great hall in the shape of a cross, the center of which holds a 50-ft tall idol of Albia. The goddess appears as a tall woman wearing long robes, her hair piled on her head and clasped with a tiara. She holds a long, oval shield in her left hand and a sword in her right hand drags behind her. The goddess has no eyes, but does have a massive carbuncle (20,000 gp) set in her forehead.

The remainder of the cathedral is taken up by what are, in essence, four towers, each a fortress in and of itself. The cross-shaped great hall lies between these fortresses. The towers have crenellated tops patrolled by crossbowmen in mail and white tunics and pyramidal roofs that rise 30 feet and are clad in green copper. The great hall between them has an arched roof clad in stained glass, the glass bathing the floor of the hall and the idol in a kaleidoscope of colors.

Each tower hosts a brotherhood of knights – the northern host, the southern host, the eastern host and the western host. Each host consists of a company of men-at-arms in plate mail and carrying shield, mace and throwing hammer. Each host is commanded by a high priest – Aeton of the north, Sigur of the south, Haeln of the east and Fadis of the south. These four men, all brothers, were raised in the Albian church and are the grandsons of Mael the Holy, a cleric that worked his entire life to construct this magnificent temple. The youngest of them is now 60 years old.

Despite their holy vows, the brothers are quarrelsome and often petty in their behavior to one another. The three youngest resent Sigur, who keeps the remains of their ancestors in a crypt beneath his fortress, allowing none to enter and pay their respects in fear of thievery (he says). The crypt of the ancestors holds a tapestry depicting Albia standing astride a red dragon. The golden tiara on Albia's head in the tapestry is woven of golden thread. If that thread is removed from the tapestry and placed in a pile at the foot of her idol, it transforms into a crown that confers the powers of a *girdle of storm giant strength*. The four brothers are unaware of this crown's existence.

Aeton, Cleric Lvl 7: HP 26; AC 1 [18]; Save 9 (7 vs. paralysis and poison); CL/XP 8/800; Special: Banish undead, spells (2/2/2/1/1). Platemail, shield, war hammer, holy symbol.

Fadis, Cleric Lvl 8: HP 26; AC 2 [17]; Save 8 (6 vs. paralysis and poison); CL/XP 9/1100; Special: Banish undead, spells (2/2/2/2/2). Platemail, heavy mace, holy symbol, brass necklace (100 gp).

Haeln, Cleic Lvl 6: HP 25; AC 1 [18]; Save 10 (8 vs. paralysis and poison); CL/XP 7/600; Special: Banish undead, spells (2/2/1/1). Platemail, shield, light mace, throwing hammer, holy symbol.

Sigur, Cleric Lvl 9: HP 23; AC 1 [18]; Save 7 (5 vs. paralysis and poison); CL/XP 10/1400; Special: Banish undead, spells (3/3/3/2/2). Platemail, shield, light mace, holy symbol, brass armband (900 gp).

1624.

Slakethirst is a bustling town of rowdies known for its fighting pits and numerous lodges of rangers, brave men and women who patrol the wilderness in defense of human civilization. The town has walls of stone and wood, with a maze-like interior. The fields around Slakethirst are grown with lavender, woad, madder, ting and flax. These fields support the town's textile and dye industries. The town has wider streets than Amistie or Hofn, with brightly painted buildings and chains hung with lanterns spanning the streets. Slakethirst is the home port of Bonny Prince Andus' pirate fleet.

The town is ruled by an elected council of aldermen who elect a speaker. The current speaker is Frede Mondo, a lecherous dyer with deep ties to the city's rampant criminal element. He has turned the speaker's manor into a meeting place for thieves, grifters and ladies of ill repute, nicknamed by him the League of Pilferers.

Opposing Frede is a retired soldier and friend of the people, Salum Kayne. Salum is a heavy-set man with a rugged, scarred face and a bushy beard. He is a compassionate man who made his money as a fur trader after retiring as the town's under marshal many years ago. He is known for his lavish parties and for his generosity to the poor.

Salum Kayne, Fighter Lvl 7: HP 38; AC 3 [16]; Save 8; CL/XP 7/600, Special: Multiple attacks, parry. Chainmail, shield, spear, hand axe, light crossbow, malachite (900 gp).

1626.

A sun-drenched hillside here is covered with a sprawling village of small buildings covered in white plaster and tiny lanes and stairs paved in flavescent limestone. The village could house over 100 people, but has only one inhabitant, an old Sea Lord named Crazy Jack. Crazy Jack claims to have been everything from a highwayman to a pirate to the king of a southern island. He is bald as a coot, with burned, leathery skin and a missing right arm. His clothes are simple and tattered, but he has a gleaming silver sword hanging from his belt. Jack moves about in the village, sleeping where he pleases. He has a store of rum hidden in a cellar, and otherwise survives by trapping small animals and birds. His most prized possession is a glass eye that he calls Alia, and to which he has a habit of speaking. If visitors are decent to Jack, Jack is decent to them, but if threatened he does not hesitate to kill.

Crazy Jack, Fighter Lvl 12: HP 44; AC 7 [12]; Save 4; CL/XP 12/2000, Special: Multiple attacks, parry. Leather armor, short swords (2), dagger, light crossbow, bronze icon of Albia (100 gp).

1705.

There is a primordial fire pit dug into a hollow here. The fire pit holds the first fire tendered by mortals in the universe, a brilliant white flame as pure as the phlogiston. The grove of the ancient fire is surrounded by tall, straight trees with black bark and reddish leaves the size of silver dollars that seem to drift to the ground day and night, every day of the year, carpeting the forest floor. The divine fire is guarded by large crows covered in brilliant, rainbow plumage. These canny birds are as intelligent as any human (maybe more so) and they do not permit anyone within 20 feet of the divine fire save druids and lawful clerics of 9th level and higher. The fire cannot be quenched by water – attempts to do so breed 1d3+3 steam elementals that immediately leap to the defense of their mother.

The fire can be used to light torches, producing a normal flame. Bodies thrown into the fire (dead or alive) are quickly consumed and then re-emerge from the surrounding trees per the *reincarnation* spell.

Rainbow Crow: HD 8; AC 1 [18]; Atk 2 claws (1d4) and bite (1d6); Move 6 (F30); Save 8; CL/XP 11/1700; Special: +1 weapon to hit, double damage on chaotic creatures, spells (detect evil, protection from evil), magic resistance (10%).

Steam Elemental: HD 8; AC 2 [17]; Atk 1 strike (3d6); Move (F36); Save 8; CL/XP 9/1100; Special: Whirlwind, choking fumes (save inside whirlwind or unconscious for 1d4 rounds), takes wrinkles out of clothing.

1708.

At a point where three streams join the Green River there is a 12-foot tall idol of Olchies, an ancient deity of the stone giants who governed petty revenge and witty retorts. Olchies looks like a stone giant with a head that resembles a chameleon. He wears the leather harness and loinclout common to the stone giants and holds a shield in one hand and a bronze torch in the other. One can remove the torch from the statue's grasp by climbing up on his shoulder and confessing in his ear the last petty revenge they took upon a friend or loved one. The admission is immediately transmitted in indelible ink to the back of the target of that petty revenge, written in the harsh runes of the stone giants. The torch is 4-feet long and very heavy (treat as a two-handed sword for purposes of weight). The torch gives off a vibrant green glow when removed from the statue and has the following powers while in the swamp: 1) The holder is guided via a green beam to whatever object or person in the swamp seeks; 2) The person is not harmed, annoyed or molested by the animals of the swamp, including vermin; and 3) As soon as the holder has found what they sought, the torch disappears, reappearing in the hand of the idol of Olchies. If the torch is not carried into the swamp, it disappears in one hour and returns to the idol.

1718.

A fortress monastery of Albia, the White Goddess of the Sea Lords, has been erected here overlooking the sea. The monastery is made of white stone with doors of thick white oak. The monastery has four peaked towers with walls that sweep from one tower to another like rolling waves. Inside the monastery live none priests (six first level clerics and three third level clerics) in crisp white robes and leather sandals. These men defend the fishermen of the coast (as best they can) against monsters, bandits and pirates. They have a small sloop-of-war anchored in their walled harbor and maintain a garrison of twenty longbowmen adept at fighting on land and sea. The longbowmen of the monastery wear white tunics and hoods over their chainmail. The abbot is Bruth, a wise old soldier with light brown hair and sea green eyes. Heavyset, with a flat face, Bruth is straightforward and brusk with non-believers and ruthless with the wicked. The monastery holds the last surviving copy of the *Book of Twelve Dooms*, an ancient work of the priests of Albia that predicts twelve successive dooms that will befall mankind, the last being the end of the world. The sinking of the White Islands was the sixth doom.

The fortress treasury contains 1,150 gp, a store of 100 vellum scrolls, a set of brass vambraces (worth 50 gp) and four rainbow crow feathers (worth 25 gp each).

Bruth, Cleric Lvl 9: HP 29; AC 1 [18]; Save 7 (5 vs. paralysis and poison); CL/XP 10/1400; Special: Banish undead, spells (3/3/3/2/2). Platemail, shield, light mace, sling, holy symbol.

1723.

Peric is a slender man with fine, white hair and coal-black eyes that smolder when one catches him unawares. A lord in his own right, he dwells in a concentric castle of gray stone that sits near the sea. The castle has a fortified harbor and Peric owns a lion ship and crews it with hobgoblins in full helms and thick cloaks (to hide their identities). A hamlet of 200 goblins dwells within the castle walls.

The castle is surrounded by wondrous orchards and gardens. Water is drawn from a large well at the foot of the castle mound. A magical stone is sunk deep within this well, and this stone not only charges the well water (one drink in six acts as a random magic potion), but also increases the caster level of all the folk in the immediate vicinity. Those who cannot cast spells gain the ability to cast a single magic-user spell within the castle walls.

Peric pines away for his lover from the sea. The strange woman bore him twins with porcelain skin and large, blue-grey eyes – a boy and a girl who rarely speak and who give most folks the creeps by their mere presence. To find their mother, who disappeared six years ago, Peric has hired Crathe, a wizened old crone who seems to appear and disappear as she likes. When present, she dwells in the dungeons beneath the castle, working on her spells and, rumor has it, consorting with demons.

Peric's treasure consists of 1,460 gp, a collection of sixteen silver cups (worth 10 gp each), a banded agate worth 400 gp and seven head of oxen with dark blue coats (worth 30 gp each).

Peric, Fighting-Man Lvl 9: HP 36; AC 3 [16]; Save 6; CL/XP 9/1100, Special: Multiple attacks, parry. Chainmail, shield, long sword, dagger, light crossbow.

Crathe, Magic-User Lvl 7: HP 18; AC 9 [10]; Save 9 (7 vs. spells); CL/XP 7/600; Special: Spells (4/3/2/1). Staff, dagger, darts (5), spellbook.

1729.

A band of eight traveling dancers from the south has made their way to this spot on their journey north. The dancers are tall and lithe, almost gaunt, with muscular legs and otherwise somewhat androgynous bodies. They have wavy hair of dark blonde, hazel eyes and tan skin. The women of the band, numbering five, paint their faces with broad, white bands from forehead to chin. All of them decorate themselves with brightly colored glass beads and strips of coeurl hide taken from the southern jungles they call home. The dancers are acrobatic and quick, and in battle they are almost unsurpassed. They seek a prophesied spiritual leader and oracle that happens to resemble one of the party members.

Southern Dancers, Monk Lvl 5: HP 5d4; AC 5 [14]; Save 11; CL/XP 4/120; Special: Weaponless damage (1d10), weapon damage +2, move 16, deadly strike (75% stun, 25% kill), only surprised on 1 in 6, deflect missiles, climb walls 89%, delicate tasks 35%, hear sounds 4 in 6, hide in shadows 30%, move silently 40%, open locks 30%, slow fall 20 ft, speak with animals, mastery of silence.

1812.

A compact castle of granite blocks with walls painted in murals depicting the surrounding countryside – a camouflage that actually makes it as difficult for travelers to notice the castle as it is to notice a secret door. The castle overlooks a sparkling bay thronged by small caves that are home to holy hermits, men dedicated to spiritual perfection through want and protected by the owner of the castle, the wizard known as the Grey Vision.

The Gray Vision, Marvis to his friends, is a slight man who dresses as a commoner, tending the castle grounds and scrubbing the murals to keep them clean. As a commoner, Marvis wears crimson breeches and a loose doublet of beige cloth, soiled from hard labor, and soft boots. In his guise as the Grey Vision, Marvis wears heeled boots, a wig of auburn ringlets (heavily perfumed), and silk and lace finery of warm, cinereous tones and jewelry of Jovian silver. Despite his simple disguise and seemingly benevolent attitude to the monks of Albia, the Gray Vision intends to extend his dominion over all other magicians of the coast, destroying any who come close to achieving his level of expertise.

The Grey Vision's treasure includes 955 gp in a heavy, locked trunk, a light mace gilded with white gold (worth 65 gp), a veil of hepatizon chain (worth 15 gp) and 10 pounds of cashews stored in a terracotta jar in his pantry (worth 20 gp per pound).

Grey Vision, Magic-User Lvl 11: HP 23; AC 9 [10]; Save 5 (3 vs. spells); CL/XP 11/1700; Special: Spells (4/4/4/3/3). Staff, dagger (3), spellbook.

1814.

Remains of an old stone giant quarry lies near the shore. The walls of the quarry tower overhead 100 to 150 feet high, and portions are filled with up to 10 feet of water. An ancient oktomon scholar, as wicked as he is wise, dwells in these waters, engraving his knowledge on the stone floor of the quarry. He keeps a treasure of 1,200 gp, a pair of dangly gold earrings set with orc fangs (worth 100 gp), the bones of an elven war chief dipped in purple wax (the head is stuffed with hops and holds a sphere of alabaster containing a treasure map) in a tarnished bronze box.

Oktomon: HD 3; AC 6 [13]; Atk Up to 4 strikes (1d3); Move 12 (Swim 18); Save 14; CL/XP 7/600; Special: Encyclopedic knowledge of the coast's history and the mythology of his own people and the stone giants, casts spells as a 7th level druid, can cast two spells per round.

1901.

The northern portion of this hex is the range of a giant lynx. Like all of its mystic kind, it can cast divinations for those who earn its trust, and it can produce garnets by urinating in small holes that it digs in its territory. These garnets are especially valued by magic-users for experiments and researches into divination. The giant lynx dwells beneath a rocky ledge in the deepest portion of the woodlands. It has at least 20 garnets buried in its territory, and might be convinced to lead people to these gems.

Giant Lynx: HD 2; AC 6[13]; Atk 2 claws (1d2), 1 bite (1d4); Move 12; Save 16; CL/XP 2/30; Special: Rear claws, spells (1/day - locate object, commune, legend lore (about the forest only), detect invisibility.

1903.

A long rift in the landscape is home to the holding of a large hobgoblin tribe, the Withered Hand by name. The walls of the rift are 40 feet tall and riddled with the mines and long burrows of the hobgoblins. The hobgoblins organize themselves into warrior bands, each led by a chieftain who answers to the warlord Zriek Long-Shanks. The rift floor supports a forest of mighty oaks from which the hobgoblins draw wood for their weapons and homes. They use the surrounding woods for fuel for their smelters, which are located in a deep pit beneath the rift, venting through a clever series of chimneys to the outside world.

The hobgoblins dig cobalt, iron, sulfur and arsenic from their mines and make use of all of it. Their weapons are made of an alloy of iron and cobalt and they dip their arrows in powdered arsenic (kept in the bottom of the quivers). Their burrows are located above the mines and are decorated with tile murals of great battles and cruel victories. The entrances to the burrows are guarded by large, shaggy mastiffs that attack as wolves.

The hobgoblins dress in woolens of purple and yellow plaid, with baggy shirts and leather bracers on their arms. They are never without their short bows and swords, but in battle dress in scale armor and carry axes and war hammers. They value puissance at arms and poetry, and recite long sagas in gravelly voices to the accompaniment of iron chimes. Their shields are decorated with twelve pointed stars.

Zriek, Hobgoblin Warlord: HD 7; AC 2 [17]; Atk 1 weapon (1d8+1); Move 9; Save 9; CL/XP 7/600; Special: None.

1922.

A mile-long sandbar lies in wait in the hex, lurking beneath the waves to entrap passing ships. The sandbar is alive and sentient. Ships that are entrapped are then attacked by six sandlings, extensions of the sandbar. If all of the sandlings are destroyed, the sandbar sinks back beneath the waves, apparently defeated, though in fact nothing short of magically turning it to stone will destroy the monstrosity.

Sandling: HD 4; AC 3 [16]; Atk 1 bite (1d8); Move 12 (B9); Save 13; CL/XP 5/240; Special: Resistance to edged weapons (50%).

1924.

Old Neefe is a man of great and mysterious talents. Once a reaver of the coast, he has retired to a small red castle nestled on a gentle rise that overlooks the grand sweep of the sea. Neefe now works as a bounty hunter. In his castle he keeps a kennel for his hunting hounds, an aerie for his falcons and a shrine of white marble and gold dedicated to Albia. Underneath a slab in this shrine he hides his sea chest, full of loot and the clothes and weapons he once used as a pirate.

Neefe is a fine-boned man with gray eyes, close-cropped hair of dark brown kissed with silver. He has a heavy, plain face heavily scarred from a life of battle. Devious and flirtatious, he usually wears a burgundy cotton waistcoat and short, black trousers with tall boots. He has a treasure of 2,500 sp, 1,200 gp, eight porcelain vases depicting gruesome executions (worth 75 gp each) and a silver great helm (worth 100 gp).

Under the protection of Neefe's holding there is a village of dwarves, outcasts from the south with light brown skin, curly red to reddish-brown hair and steel grey eyes. These dwarves keep smallish blue cattle from whose milk they produce many excellent cheeses. One dwarf, an elder male named Edwen, is skilled as an apothecary. With a month's notice and the proper ingredients, he can brew a healing draught (potion of healing) or make an ointment that cures blindness.

Old Neefe, Half-Orc Thief 10: HP 23; AC 6 [13]; Save 7 (5 vs. devices and disease); CL/XP 9/1100; Special: Darkvision, back stab x5, climb walls 94%, delicate tasks 70%, hear sounds 5 in 6, hide in shadows 65%, move silently 70%, open locks 65%, read languages, read magic writings. Leather armor, shield, hand axe, daggers (4), darts (6), short bow, thieves' tools.

1931.

The hilltop here has been cleared of timber and now plays host to five tall windmills. The windmills are built of wood and owned by a brotherhood of lustful wind priests. The priests line their windmill's blades with nets strung with carnelians and coated with honey. These strange nets are designed to capture passing sylphs, who are attracted by the sound of Aeolian wind harps. Once captured, they are bound in dainty iron chains and kept in luxurious captivity, the priests pleading with them daily for a kiss or kind word, reciting passionate poetry and offering every treasure they can lay their hands on. The sylphs are, of course, adamant in their refusals, and wish only to be freed. In their quest for treasures rare and wondrous, the priests are not above luring adventurers into their windmills and then killing them.

Wind Priests: HD 4; AC 9 [10]; Atk 1 (1d6 or weapon or spell); Move 12; Save 13; CL/XP 6/400; Special: Shape change (usually into birds), cast spells as 6th level druid.

2016.

A crumbling old lighthouse stands on the coast here. A lambent, golden glow drifts from the top of the beacon tower beneath a dome of thick, cloudy glass. The beacon tower has a locked iron door. Patches of otherworldly slime coat the white stones of the tower. Behind the iron door there is a spiral stair leading up to a living chamber of a scholarly young mage named Airn. Airn has a cot, a few bits of clothing hanging on pegs and a desk atop which there is an ornate box of ebony and brass covered with a myriad of dials and knobs. Each night, he can be found hunched over that machine communicating with a scholar from a far world via a golden beam that strikes the glass dome of the beacon tower. Over the past few nights, something else has been attracted by that beam – creatures that look like a large, black sea stars with oily, rubbery skin on their backs and yellowish, spiky skin underneath, with faces that consist of a single, glossy black eye and a slit mouth from which they can protrude a bony feeding tube. These creatures slink up from the sea at night and climb up the tower, looking for a way inside. Airn has recently become aware of them and he is terrified. His friend from afar, a man called Am-Or, claims he can send down a golden beam that will transport Airn to safety, but he worries. On the night of a visit from the adventurers, the star things will attack the tower in force, with no fewer than 30 of the creatures doing their best to eat through the door.

Star Thing: HD 3; AC 4 [15]; Atk 2 strikes (1d4 + acid); Move 9 (C9); Save 14 (12 vs. spells); CL/XP 6/400; Special: Acid touch causes 1d6 damage first round, 1d4 second round, 1d3 third round and 1 damage in the fourth round unless washed away with some form of alcohol, ESP at will, immune to cold and mind effects, magic resistance (15%).

2026.

A valiant young lady of the ancient, noble blood of the Sea Lords lives here in a massive castle of dull, brown stone constructed long before the arrival of the sea lords. The castle is constructed on the shores of a shallow lake that sometimes bubbles with foul gases that emerge from the muck. The lady, Acenn, rules over a sparsely populated domain rich in horses. Aside from many small, stone cottages and gardens of currants, cabbages, maize and vile borage, the manorial village boasts a seedy tavern called the Finger-In-Eye. The tavern serves corn beer and golden mushroom soup and is an excellent place to meet the kind of ne'er-do-wells one might hire to venture into a dungeon. Her treasure is kept in a locked chest (with a poison gas trap) and contains 1,020 gp, a wooden box of balm (heals 1 hp if applied at night, 20 uses) and four large topaz (worth 100 gp each). She has a *broom of flying* next to her bed.

Acenn, Fighter Lvl 10: HP 45; AC 1 [18]; Save 5; CL/XP 10/1400, Special: Multiple attacks, parry. Platemail, shield, hand axe, dagger, longbow, copper bracelets set with hematites (worth 40 gp each).

2106.

A flooded sea cave here sends random bursts of coruscating light out onto the waves. This light is just barely noticeable in the daytime (per finding secret doors), but is very apparent at night. The cave entrance is ringed by jagged stones and there is no other way in (besides magic) than repelling down the cliff face above and then dropping into the waist-high (and often surging) water. About 20 feet into the cave there is drier land and small entrance into much deeper caves. It is apparent that pirates have used this place in the past – there are old supplies here like masts and sail cloth and slimy ropes as well as the flotsam and jetsam one associates with pirates like cutlasses and leather hats. The weird lights come from the deeper caverns, and exploring them carries a small chance of being blinded. The light erupts on a roll of 1 on 1d6 and forces all with sight to make a saving throw or be blinded for 1 hour.

Most of the sea caves here are empty save for random vermin. At the very end of the cave complex there is a large, irregular cavern that houses a deep well. The stone around the well has been turned to glass of every color in the rainbow (and a few that are not). The light erupts from this well. Surrounding it, worshipping it, are a dozen slime babies – creatures that look like large, stocky, bloated infants covered in a viscous slime of crimson mixed with emerald green. These bizarre creatures scream with glee when people enter, and welcome them to their dance around the well. After a few rounds, they will attempt to push their guests to their deaths down the well.

Slime Baby: HD 4+1; AC 4 [15]; Atk 2 fists (1d6); Move 12; Save 13; CL/XP 5/240; Special: Slimy skin makes them difficult to grapple (-4), immune to water and earth magic.

2120.

The sea floor here is actually a giant impact crater – as is the land surrounding the sea. The water in the crater is cold and dark. In the middle of the crater there is the glint of a massive diamond, as large as a man's skull and worth easily 20,000 gp. The diamond is partially buried in the silt and, in fact, is in the grasp of the demon Esmarun, who fell to earth a dozen millennia ago. Taking his diamond will make him terribly cross.

Esmarun was once a powerful demon, but a severe underestimation in the power of a human wizard was his undoing. He is now a fourth-category demon with a bat-like head, a fungal ruff around his neck that makes him look like an Elizabethan gentleman, a bony, skeletal face with eyes like limpid pools of disdain, a trumpet nose and a huge, fanged mouth. It has long, feathered arms ending in clawed hands and stout legs ending in clawed feet. Esmarun has gray skin that drips with foul ichor that stinks of urine. His wings are bat-like.

Esmarun: HD 11 (51 hp); AC –1 [20]; Atk 2 claws (1d4), 1 bite (1d6+2); Move 9 (F14); Save 4; CL/XP 13/2300; Special: +1 or better magic weapon needed to hit, magic resistance (65%), +2 on to-hit rolls, immune to fire, magical abilities.

2125.

An invisible castle rests here, overlooking the pounding surf. The castle is situated among the jagged rocks of the coast, and might only be discerned by a sea bird crashing into it unawares, or by the off shape of the waves. The architects of the invisible castle are unknown, but the interior (which is visible) is filled with sweeping arches and smooth, unadorned stonework. Cords of crimson and gold hang in all the archways and the floor is composed of speckled pebbles. Most of the rooms are empty save for black candle stubs, bits of broken weapons and splintered shields and conical fur caps matted with blood.

The castle has a single domed tower in its center, reachable by a narrow stair protected by an elder air elemental called Reserach. Reserach knows not to attack any who holds a lit black candle. At the top of the stairs there is a small chamber covered by the aforementioned dome, which is clear as glass but as sturdy as adamant. On the floor of the chamber there is a strange device of polished (and now tarnished) brass. The device is conical, with a loop on the point. If the device is polished and held against a point on the glass dome for two minutes, a beam of focused sunlight bursts from the dome in the direction indicated. This beam does 10d6 points of damage to anything it hits and causes even green foliage to burst into flame after three minutes of exposure.

Reserach, Air Elemental: HD 12 (66 hp); AC 2 [17]; Atk 1 strike (2d8); Move (F36); Save 3; CL/XP 13/2300; Special: Whirlwind.

2201.

A rust-red creek flows from a cave in a hillside to an old crater. The crater has an island in the middle that is always covered in snow and ice. The island is about 3/4 of a mile long and 1/2 a mile wide and forms a ridge, with the heights about 80 feet above the level of the red water that fills the crater. The water is about 40 feet deep at its deepest.

A sage named Damanar (he calls himself "the Prophet") dwells on the island as a hermit. Exploring the island many years ago, he discovered a strange metal pyramid set in a hollow. The pyramid is actually composed of four smaller pyramids. Three pyramids, colored red, blue and yellow, form the base, while a white pyramid is stacked on top of them. The metal of the pyramids is impervious to acid and fire, and when struck with lightning it sucks the heat from the surrounding air at an even faster rate than it already does, causing damage equal to the lightning bolt to all creatures within 60 feet of the pyramid. Damanar claims that the pyramids, the "conclave" as he calls them, speak to him in his mind, and have opened his eyes to the universe.

Damanar the Prophet: HD 4 (24 hp); AC 7 [12]; Atk 1 staff (1d4); Move 12; Save 13; CL/XP 5/240; Special: Spells (1/ day each – prismatic spray, prismatic sphere, prismatic wall, rainbow pattern). These new spells can be found at the end of this volume.

2203.

The woods here are rife with decapus – terrestrial squids that swing from branch to branch in the fashion of monkeys. The decapus are simple hunters. They are encountered on a roll of 1-3 on 1d6 in groups of 1d4+3. Each day spent in this hex carries with it a 1 in 6 chance of a powerful rumbling that shakes the branches of trees. This rumbling is caused by a large machine buried beneath the soil. The machine is complex beyond the reckoning of most folk – perhaps very high-level magic-users could suss out the workings – and the machine is in poor condition. It is powered by a geothermal vent and was designed as a power unit for other machinery that has long since disappeared.

Decapus: HD 4; AC 4 [15]; Atk 9 tentacles (1d4); Move 6 (C12); Save 13; CL/XP 7/600; Special: Strangle (tentacle that beats AC by 6 or more latches on for 1d4 damage per round, even 6 rounds after death), phantasmal force.

2223.

There is a small island here of sandy beaches and golden grasses on rolling hills. Those who step on the island soon forget who they are, where they are and why they are. The second a foot touches the land its owner must pass a saving throw or be struck with amnesia. Each hour spent on the island requires a new save for those unaffected at a cumulative -1 penalty. A person well prepared who recites their name and parentage over and over gains a +5 bonus to save.

At the island's center there is a golden bowl on a tripod. The bowl is guarded by a golden boar of immense proportions and terrible temper. The bowl contains a portion of ichor, the very lifeblood of the gods. The mere touch of the ichor inflicts 9d6 points of damage on a person. Tasting it causes a person to burst into flames from the inside out, killing them and reducing them to ash in less than a minute.

Golden Boar: HD 7; AC 4 [15]; Atk 1 gore (2d8); Move 15; Save 9; CL/XP 8/800; Special: +1 or better weapon to hit, immune to fire and cold.

2226.

Tall cliffs along the coast are covered in the writings of the stone giants. These writings tell the history and mythology of the stone giant kingdom. The cliffs are a good source of ancient legends, but they are weathered and readers have only a 1% chance per hour of study of uncovering useful information.

2314.

This coast is littered with clumps of dozing sea cats. Jagged rocks rise from the pounding surf, and between them there are glass-domed houses. Inside these houses there are stone pillars that descend into the sea. Atop each pillar there is a pot of earth holding an orchid. One can only get into one of these greenhouses by swimming 15 feet under the water surface and then up into the structure, which is steamy and terribly warm. By climbing up the 6-ft pillar, one can catch the scent of a golden orchid, which heals all wounds and cures all diseases. Attempting to pilfer an orchid or damaging one brings down the wrath of the gods in the form of a movanic deva with fiery eyes, long tongues as red as blood, hawk talons on their feet and wielding solar axes.

Movanic Deva: HD 8; AC -1 [20]; Atk 1 weapon (3d6); Move 18 (F36, S36); Save 8; CL/XP 15/2900; Special: +1 or better weapon to hit, magic resistance (55%), wields a +1 flaming axe, never attacked by animals, shift between planes at will, spells: anti-magic shell x3, continual light, cure disease, cure light wounds x7, detect evil, dispel magic, invisibility (self), plane shift, polymorph self, protection from normal missiles and remove curse.

2329.

A circle of white stones, crudely carved and heavily weathered stands on a promontory overlooking the sea. On the nights of the full moon, it is visited by a pod of five orcaweres. The orcas were once stone giants who deigned worship the gods of chaos. Their transgressions brought upon them this curse – that save under the light of a full moon they should be banished from the cold, solid earth of their birth into the primordial abyss of the sea. At the full moon, the poor souls assume stone giant shape and crawl up out of the sea to plea for their souls at the old stone circle. Years of the curse have driven them nearly to madness, and they tend to behave violently toward intruders in the circle. When the moon is not full, there is a 3 in 6 chance that they will be hunting off the coast in whale form.

Orcaware: HD 12; AC 3 [16]; Atk 1 weapon (2d8) or bite (2d6); Move 12 (S18); Save 3; CL/XP 13/2300; Special: Can only be killed with a silver weapon.

2331.

The strange men of the Last Kingdom, located to the south of the included map, have an outpost here. The outpost is a square fortress with 40-ft tall walls that are 10 to 15 feet thick. The interior walls are lined with block houses, simple and Spartan, composed of glossy black bricks. These block houses are four stories tall and Spartan in their furnishings, save for the richly decorated wall hangings.

In the middle of the fortresses courtyard there is a round tower. 60 feet tall, in which the commandant, Iolt, dwells. Iolt is brave and, like many of the Last Men, suspicious and xenophobic. She has olive skin and blonde hair cropped in a page boy cut. Iolt's sergeant is Shad, an aggressive man with no sense of humor. Iolt communicates with her liege via a large crystal (worth 100 gp) set in a matrix of gold wires secured to the walls. The crystals give off a strange hum in various tones that Iolt can interpret.

The fortress houses forty men-at-arms. Twenty of the men-at-arms wear ring armor and carry heavy crossbows and short swords. The others wear chainmail and carry shield and long sword.

2424.

Gaen, the Triton Prince of the Coast dwells here in a great mount of reddish-black basalt with towers and spiraling battlements carved into the exterior and a maze-like interior guarded by domesticated moray eels. The tunnels lead to caverns richly appointed in precious metals and statuary. One particularly large cavern that is entered from above holds a great marble statue of a sea demon – a terrible beast that is an unwholesome mélange of whale, jellyfish and goat. A large spear juts from the creature's chest, and it grasps it with its tentacle arms, as though it was frozen in stone while trying to dislodge the weapon.

Gaen is voluminous triton with a great shock of white hair, a long beard decorated with purple-shelled mollusks, ice blue eyes that can practically freeze a man in his path with a hard stare and powerful arms that hold two barbed shafts that look to have once been attached to harpoons. In battle, he wears a coat of shagreen scales ornamented with bronze bolts and gold trim and a bronze helm in the ancient Greek style with a crest of urchin spines. Gaen commands a rich tribute in precious metals and stones from the ships that ply the coast.

The prince has a royal guard of 10 triton warriors. He rules a population of 200 merfolk. Their holdings are rich in capricorns (goat-fish), the merfolk weaving their wool into magical shawls that protect one from the cold (resistance to cold weather, half damage from cold spells and effects).

Giant Moray Eel: HD 4; AC 7 [12]; Atk 1 bite (2d6); Move 0 (S9); Save 13; CL/XP 4/120; Special: None.

Triton: HD 3; AC 5 [14]; Atk 1 trident (1d8+1); Move 1 (S18); Save 14; CL/XP 4/120; Special: Magic resistance (90%).

Gaen, Triton Prince: HD 6 (32 hp); AC 5 [14]; Atk 2 harpoons (1d8+1); Move 1 (S18); Save 11; CL/XP 8/800; Special: Magic resistance (90%), cast spells as 6th level magic-user.

2507.

This hex contains an island of mist-shrouded swamps and rocky coasts. The coasts are inhabited by numerous cyclops. These giants are encountered in groups of 1d3 on rolls of 1-2 on 1d6. In the swampy interior of the island, tall hills poke up from the mists, some of them large enough to support small villages. These villages are inhabited by sisterhoods of 1d20+30 amazons. The amazons are tall and handsome women, with strong noses and gray eyes. They wear blood red silks and glass bangles on their wrists and ankles.

A large plateau in the center of the island holds a natural depression that serves as a stadium for competitions decreed by the patron goddess of the island, Weonau. Weonau is the wild goddess of evil who appears as an athletic maiden with a bony crest atop her head and running down her back, beady eyes of alabaster white and black, scaled skin. She carries two throwing knives, nicknamed Lust and Anger. Her idol is placed in the middle of the stadium and stands 20 feet tall. The stadium stands above two interlocking arches that cover a fire pit.

Once each year, the seven best warriors of each amazon village meet to fight in this stadium for the honor of bearing the sacred black flame of the goddess. The current holder of the flame walks into the fire pit beneath the idol of the goddess, where she is consumed by the black flames. Once this has occurred, the amazons fight (rarely to the death) to determine the island's champion. This champion then walks (or crawls) into the fire pit where she absorbs the flame. The holder of the black flame gains the spellcasting abilities of a 7th level cleric and the touch attack of a wight. The current champion of the amazons is Brighda.

Cyclops: HD 8+2; AC 4 [15]; Atk 1 weapon (2d8); Move 12; Save 8; CL/XP 9/1100; Special: Throw boulders at -2 to hit, surprised on roll of 1-3 on 1d6, immune to fire.

Amazon: HD 1+1; AC 5 [14]; Atk 1 weapon (1d8+1); Move 12; Save 17; CL/XP 1/15; Special: Fight as a berserker.

Brighda, Cleric Lvl 7: HP 30; AC 5 [14]; Save 9 (7 vs. paralysis and poison); CL/XP 10/1400; Special: Control undead, spells (2/2/2/1/1), touch drains level as wight, can fight as berserker. Chainmail, flanged mace, unholy symbol.

2511.

A trio of nymphs dance here in a peaceful meadow, caressing the stones with their feet and pleasing the earth with their gentle grace. The nymphs dance for approximately one hour at dawn and again at dusk. Those who witness the dance may be struck blind (save to negate), but they also have their wounds healed and their diseases cured. The rest of the day is spent at rest and play. While the nymphs are not entirely defenseless, ten giant beetles lurk just beneath the ground, ready to attack when needed.

Nymph: HD 3; AC 9 [10]; Atk none; Move 12; Save 14; CL/XP 5/240; Special: Sight causes blindness or death.

Giant Beetle (5ft): HD 3; AC 3 [16]; Atk 1 bite (3d6); Move 9; Save 14; CL/XP 4/120; Special: None.

2513.

Hofn is a Sea Lord town surrounded by a stone wall with a large, wooden gate. The town was founded about a century ago, when the Sea Lords first reached the shores of the Pirate Coast. Hofn was the first of the Sea Lord towns to prosper and the first to build a stone wall in place of its original wooden palisade. The layout inside Hofn is a chaotic jumble of narrow lanes and winding stairs ascending the sides of the river valley. It is primarily known for its society of alchemists, the Chimeric Brothers, its fine, cobbled streets (laid down overnight by a wonder worker who promised to return in 100 years to claim his price, the town's children – that was about 100 years ago) and its breweries and distilleries, not to mention the taverns that distribute their wondrous wares. The town's guardsmen are virtually a law unto themselves, each constable attaining his position by paying a fee to the lord mayor and then doing their best to recoup the fee via a competitive protection racket. This overbearing law enforcement keeps crime low (or at least shifts crime into the official sphere), but makes navigating the streets of Hofn tricky for visitors.

In all, Hofn is a friendly town. It makes its living on trade, both from riches delivered by the pirate fleet of Randar the Red, and from explorers looting the interior of the country. The town is surrounded by farms and orchards of cherry and apple trees. The buildings in the town are a mixture of wattle-and-daub and wooden sideboard construction, all with shuttered windows painted with mystic glyphs meant to keep away the spirits that haunt the tortured coast.

Hofn is governed by Arles Comger, a wealthy priest of Albia whose fiery sermons and manly defense of the city against a recent onslaught of ghouls, made him the people's favorite as lord mayor. Arles detests chaos and demands order – for now, this is playing well with the people, though the innately chaotic Sea Lords will almost certainly rebel sooner or later. His chief rival is Shawna Brethad, scion of a noble house who finds the common folk irritating and Arles particularly so. Shawna has many influential friends among the seedier folk of Hofn. She is usually to be found weaving her webs from the Three Knuckles roadhouse by the town's west gate. Adventurers may find themselves in conflict with Galie Thien, an ally of Shawna and a noble woman in her own right. Galie is a flamboyant woman who is deadly quick with a blade.

Arles Comger, Cleric Lvl 7: HP 20; AC 7 [12]; Save 9 (7 vs. paralysis and poison); CL/XP 8/800; Special: Banish undead, spells (2/2/2/1/1). Leather armor, light mace, holy symbol, brass chain (55 gp).

Galie Thien, Assassin Lvl 6: HP 19; AC 6 [13]; Save 10; CL/XP 5/240; Special: Disguise, poison, backstab x2, climb walls 88%, delicate tasks 30%, hear sounds 4 in 6, hide in shadows 25%, move silently 35%, open locks 25%. Leather armor, shield, long sword, daggers (3), darts (10), vials of poison (3).

2521.

This volcanic island is covered with ridges of basalt, the valleys home to twisted and stunted black oaks. Two competing cults, that of the sister goddesses Esdis of the Sun and Zabeth of the Forge, are forced to live in an uneasy peace, the island being divided between them. The eastern half of the island contains the great temple of Zabeth and a number of old iron mines that still produce an uncommonly pure ore. The western half of the island is given over to the sun goddess and her temple in the midst of a great fishing village.

Zapeth appears as a voluptuous old woman with thickly muscled arms, large red eyes, golden skin and wearing a jack-of-plates and a thick leather apron. Tales tell of her often taking the shape of a red fox, and images of red foxes decorate her temples and many of the houses on the island. Esdis is a short, angular woman with solar spikes emanating from her head, orange eyes and vermillion skin. She wears a cloth-of-gold robe and carries two discs.

The people of the forge have the golden skin and muscled bodies of their goddess, while the people of the sun have the vermillion skin and angular features of their goddess. Each temple holds a magical fountain, the drinking of which changes one's appearance into that of the people of the forge or sun, and unless they pass a save orients their mind to the zealous worship of the same goddess.

2602.

There is a small tower here near a sparkling stream. The banks of the stream support sycamores and daffodils. The tower made of concrete (or to most folk a smooth, gray stone) and sealed with a small, metal door. The tower is 16 feet tall and about 8 feet in diameter. The interior consists of a single room that is furnished with a cramped collection of wooden furniture, all highly ornamented, including a large bear rug, the head of which has both human and bear characteristics. The tower is the home of Porkill, a perspicacious litte gnome. Porkill is a sailor and fisherman by trade, keeping a little coracle down by the stream. He waits in his tower for the return of his love, Reida, who journeyed across the Aderumdoc Mountains to visit her uncle.

Porkill: HD 2; AC 8 [11]; Atk 1 weapon (1d4); Move 6; Save 16; CL/XP 3/60; Special: Phantasmal force 1/day.

2604.

A sheltered harbor here is the mustering point of a grand fleet of pirates – the combined fleets of Randar the Red, Ydence Longshanks and Bonny Prince Andus. Their lion-prowed galleys are drawn up on the beaches and a number of temporary lean-tos and tents have been erected, and there is a larger permanent log house as well. The long house is now housing the war council of the assembled captains. The fleet is gathering here for an invasion of Bucrania. They have already made some forays into the sea, returning with much treasure and a few captives, including Llenda, the lady-in-waiting of Princess Katlithimeina. Llenda has convinced them that she is her mistress, and has made promises to Andus that he could share her throne if only he will kill her cruel father.

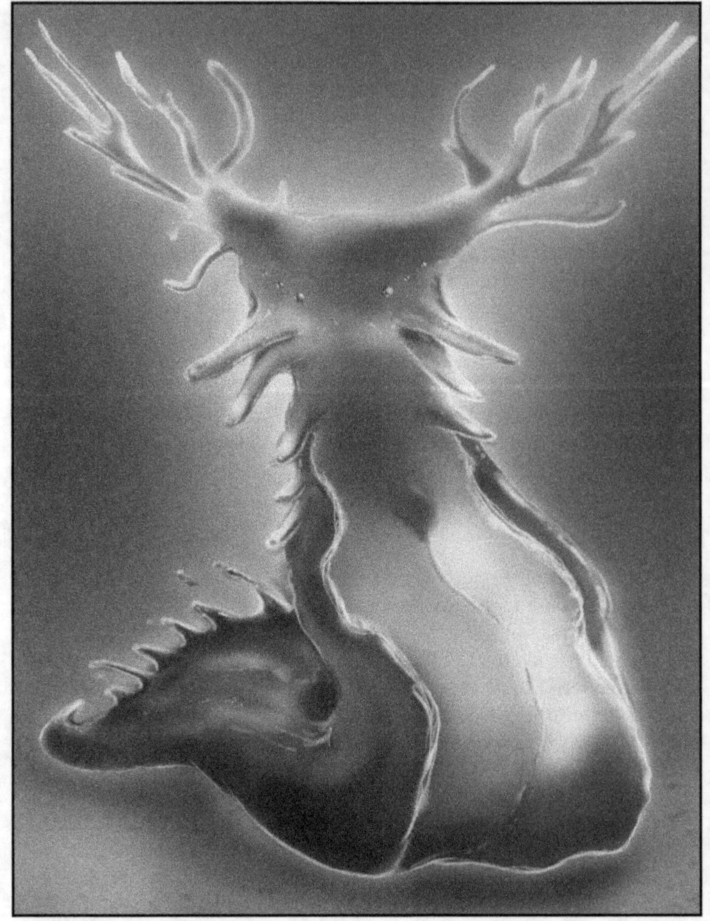

2612.

An ordinary cave set among the pines looks down on the coast. Giant sea slugs rise from the ocean and crawl up to this cave, entering it and traveling into its depths when they know they are about to die. What becomes of these creatures in the depths is unknown, but no corpses are ever found. Encounters with the slugs near or inside the cave occur on a roll of 1-2 on 1d6.

Giant Sea Slug: HD 12; AC 8 [11]; Atk 1 bite (1d12) or acid squirt; Move 6; Save 3; CL/XP 13/2300; Special: Spit acid.

2629.

There is a smallish island here. The island has a thin, acidic soil that supports a few small cherry trees. The shores of the island are cliffs and have been carved into battlements and unevenly spaced towers. These battlements are haunted by warrior shades, sailors who lost their lives in the dangerous straits and found their souls bound to the island. There is one entrance through these battlements – a stone stair that ends in a quay with moorings for up to five boats. At each new moon, a coven of five forlarren, the children of the nymph Wilfrun and the archdevil Samon, meet here to pay respects to their mother and to spit on the image of their father, which is carved into a small pillar of basalt at the island's center. The only other inhabitants of the island are venomous serpents. Each hour on the island carries a 1 in 6 chance of encountering 1d3 vipers.

Shade: HD 3+3; AC 7 [12]; Atk 1 touch (1d4 + strength drain); Move 12; Save 14; CL/XP 4/120; Special: Drain 1 point str with hit, hit only by magic weapons.

Forlarren: HD 3; AC 2 [17]; Atk 2 strikes (1d4); Move 12; Save 14; CL/XP 4/120; Special: Heat metal.

2718.

This wide island is heavily creased with green valleys and buff-colored, rocky bluffs. The valleys are planted with crops of sugar beets, huckleberries and wheat. The village holds a bizarre city-state of stone buildings like small shell keeps. Each of these towers has a fire pit in the courtyard and is inhabited by a strange creature called vindlu. The vindlu look like lithe lions covered with silvery scales. Their paws resemble human hands and though they often choose to walk on all fours, they are capable of sitting on their haunches and working with their fore-hands.

The vindlu's island is currently under the domination of an army from the Last Kingdom to the south. The Last Men are overbearing and paranoid, and both despised and tolerated by the vindlu. The vindlu number about 450 and the men-at-arms of the Last Kingdom about 200, including crossbowmen, swordsmen and swift cavalry.

The tallest and largest building on the island is a tower-shaped temple dedicated to a deity the vindlu call the Ancient Sun. The interior of the temple is clad in yellow tiles, the floor taken up with a pit of burning oil and multiple balconies for worshipers to roar their love of the great idol – a giant automaton with golden skin that glows hotter as the roars grow louder. When the vindlu have finally had enough of the xenophobic Last Men, they will release their clockwork god upon them.

Idol of the Ancient Sun: HD 15 (52 hp); AC 2 [17]; Atk 2 slams (3d6); Move 12; Save 3; CL/XP 16/3200; Special: Cone of heat (90' long and 30' wide, inflicts damage equal to the idol's initial hit points).

Vindlu: HD 1; AC 7 [12]; Atk 2 claws (1d4) and bite (1d6) or crossbow (1d6); Move 12; Save 17 (15 vs fire, death rays, traps and breath weapons); CL/XP 1/15; Special: Surprise (3 in 6).

2726.

The island here is covered by thick woodlands crossed by dark, winding rivers that taste of wine. In the center of the island there is an ancient, crumbling city-state with wooden walls 60 feet tall and large gates clad in bronze scales. The city-state is long abandoned, its treasures mostly plundered. The olive-skinned people of the island now live like wolves, wearing only wolf-pelt tunics and arming themselves with spears and slings. They return at each quarter moon to the city to pay homage to their ancient, jealous god. His idol takes the form of a great, iron gorgon crusted with sulfur. Trap doors hidden in the crumbling temple lead into ancient tunnels and pits, some of which hold ancient reliquary objects and caches of gems, and others doors into deeper caverns inhabited by twisted creatures of the underworld called the "worms that walk", creatures that are writhing conglomerations of pallid worms beneath tattered brown cloaks.

Worms That Walk: HD 4; AC 5 [14]; Atk 1 staff (1d6); Move 12; Save 13; CL/XP ; Special: Engulf victim in vermin (1d4 damage per round until a saving throw is made and then shaken for 1d4 rounds and -1 to hit and damage), can discorporate into swarm of vermin that wriggle away, cast spells as 4th level magic-user

Half-Orc Race

Half-orcs are not a race, but rather creatures with a mixture of human and humanoid (usually orc, goblin, gnoll, bugbear or hobgoblin) blood. Half-orcs can almost pass for human. They average from six to seven feet in height and are usually stocky. Their skin often has a pink, grey or green cast to it. Half-orcs often have one of the following facial features: Turned up nose, pointed ears, thick eyebrows, a heavy forehead, vestigial tusks and/or pointed teeth. Half-orc hair is coarse and unruly and usually black, dark brown or dark red. Half-orc eyes are almost always brown, brownish green or greyish green.

Half-orcs usually speak the common tongue of men and often (60%) the language of their other parent race. It is not uncommon for them to learn the language of dwarves, goblins, ogres and giants.

Half-orcs can see up to 60 feet in darkness and their sense of smell is as keen as a wolf's. Their thick skin gives them a natural Armor Class of 8 [11], which can be enhanced with armor. Half-orcs enjoy a +2 bonus to saving throws against poison and disease.

Half-orcs can advance as fighters (up to 8th level), thieves (no level limit), assassins (up to 6th level) or fighter/thieves (up to 8th level as fighter and 12th level as thief).

New Spells

Prismatic Spray

Spell Level: Magic-User, 7th Level
Range: Cone (60' long, 30' wide at base)

This spell causes seven shimmering, intertwined, multicolored beams of light to spray from your hand. Each beam has a different power. Creatures in the area of the spell with 8 HD or less are automatically blinded for 2d4 rounds. Every creature in the area is randomly struck by one or more beams, which have additional effects. Roll 1d8 for each creature in the area of effect:

Roll	Effect
1	Red causes 2d6 points of fire damage
2	Orange causes 3d6 points of acid damage
3	Yellow causes 4d6 points of electricity damage
4	Green is a deadly poison
5	Blue petrifies
6	Indigo causes insanity
7	Violet sends creatures to another plane of existence
8	Struck by two rays; roll twice on this table, re-rolling "8"s

Prismatic Wall

Spell Level: Magic-User, 8th Level
Range: 60 feet
Duration: 10 minutes/level

Prismatic wall creates a vertical wall of shimmering, multicolored light that protects from all forms of attack. The wall flashes with seven colors, each of which has a distinct power and purpose. The wall's creator can pass through and remain near the wall without harm. However, any other creature with less than 8 HD that is within 20 feet of the wall is blinded for 2d4 rounds by the colors if it looks at the wall. The wall's maximum proportions are 4 feet wide per caster level and 2 feet high per caster level. A prismatic wall spell cannot be materialized in a space occupied by a creature.

Each color in the wall has a special defense and causes damage to people passing through the wall per the colors of the *prismatic spray* spell. Red stops non-magical missiles and is negated by an *ice storm*. Orange stops magical missiles and is negated with *control winds*. Yellow stops poisons, gases and petrification and is negated with *disintegrate*. Green stops breath weapons and is negated with the *passwall* spell. Blue stops scrying and mental attacks and is negated by *magic missile*. Indigo stops all spells and is negated with a *continual light* spell. Violet is an energy field that destroys all objects and magical effects and is negated by *dispel magic*.

The wall can be destroyed, color by color, in consecutive order, by various magical effects; however, the first color must be brought down before the second can be affected, and so on. A *rod of cancellation* destroys a *prismatic wall*, but an *anti-magic shell* fails to penetrate it. *Dispel magic* cannot dispel the wall or anything beyond it. Magic resistance is effective against a *prismatic wall*, but the d% roll must be repeated for each color present.

Rainbow Pattern

Spell Level: Magic-User, 4th Level
Range: 120 feet
Duration: Concentration + 1 round/level

A glowing, rainbow-hued pattern of interweaving colors springs from a crystal prism in the magic-user's hand to fascinate those within it. Rainbow pattern fascinates a maximum of 24 Hit Dice of creatures. Creatures with the fewest HD are affected first. Among creatures with equal HD, those who are closest to the spell's point of origin are affected first. An affected creature that fails its saves is fascinated by the pattern.

With a simple gesture the pattern can be moved up to 30 feet per round. All fascinated creatures follow the pattern, trying to remain within the effect. Fascinated creatures who are restrained and removed from the pattern still try to follow it. If the pattern leads its subjects into a dangerous area each fascinated creature gets a second save. If the view of the pattern is completely blocked creatures that can't see it are no longer affected.

Hex Crawl Chronicles: The Pirate Coast is written under version 1.0a of the Open Game License. As of yet, none of the material first appearing in **Hex Crawl Chronicles: The Pirate Coast** is considered Open Game Content.

OPEN GAME LICENSE Version 1.0a

The following text is the property of Wizards of the Coast, Inc. and is Copyright 2000 Wizards of the Coast, Inc ("Wizards"). All Rights Reserved.

1. Definitions: (a)"Contributors" means the copyright and/or trademark owners who have contributed Open Game Content; (b)"Derivative Material" means copyrighted material including derivative works and translations (including into other computer languages), potation, modification, correction, addition, extension, upgrade, improvement, compilation, abridgment or other form in which an existing work may be recast, transformed or adapted; (c) "Distribute" means to reproduce, license, rent, lease, sell, broadcast, publicly display, transmit or otherwise distribute; (d)"Open Game Content" means the game mechanic and includes the methods, procedures, processes and routines to the extent such content does not embody the Product Identity and is an enhancement over the prior art and any additional content clearly identified as Open Game Content by the Contributor, and means any work covered by this License, including translations and derivative works under copyright law, but specifically excludes Product Identity. (e) "Product Identity" means product and product line names, logos and identifying marks including trade dress; artifacts; creatures characters; stories, storylines, plots, thematic elements, dialogue, incidents, language, artwork, symbols, designs, depictions, likenesses, formats, poses, concepts, themes and graphic, photographic and other visual or audio representations; names and descriptions of characters, spells, enchantments, personalities, teams, personas, likenesses and special abilities; places, locations, environments, creatures, equipment, magical or supernatural abilities or effects, logos, symbols, or graphic designs; and any other trademark or registered trademark clearly identified as Product identity by the owner of the Product Identity, and which specifically excludes the Open Game Content; (f) "Trademark" means the logos, names, mark, sign, motto, designs that are used by a Contributor to identify itself or its products or the associated products contributed to the Open Game License by the Contributor (g) "Use", "Used" or "Using" means to use, Distribute, copy, edit, format, modify, translate and otherwise create Derivative Material of Open Game Content. (h) "You" or "Your" means the licensee in terms of this agreement.

2. The License: This License applies to any Open Game Content that contains a notice indicating that the Open Game Content may only be Used under and in terms of this License. You must affix such a notice to any Open Game Content that you Use. No terms may be added to or subtracted from this License except as described by the License itself. No other terms or conditions may be applied to any Open Game Content distributed using this License.

3.Offer and Acceptance: By Using the Open Game Content You indicate Your acceptance of the terms of this License.

4. Grant and Consideration: In consideration for agreeing to use this License, the Contributors grant You a perpetual, worldwide, royalty-free, non-exclusive license with the exact terms of this License to Use, the Open Game Content.

5.Representation of Authority to Contribute: If You are contributing original material as Open Game Content, You represent that Your Contributions are Your original creation and/or You have sufficient rights to grant the rights conveyed by this License.

6.Notice of License Copyright: You must update the COPYRIGHT NOTICE portion of this License to include the exact text of the COPYRIGHT NOTICE of any Open Game Content You are copying, modifying or distributing, and You must add the title, the copyright date, and the copyright holder's name to the COPYRIGHT NOTICE of any original Open Game Content you Distribute.

7. Use of Product Identity: You agree not to Use any Product Identity, including as an indication as to compatibility, except as expressly licensed in another, independent Agreement with the owner of each element of that Product Identity. You agree not to indicate compatibility or co-adaptability with any Trademark or Registered Trademark in conjunction with a work containing Open Game Content except as expressly licensed in another, independent Agreement with the owner of such Trademark or Registered Trademark. The use of any Product Identity in Open Game Content does not constitute a challenge to the ownership of that Product Identity. The owner of any Product Identity used in Open Game Content shall retain all rights, title and interest in and to that Product Identity.

8. Identification: If you distribute Open Game Content You must clearly indicate which portions of the work that you are distributing are Open Game Content.

9. Updating the License: Wizards or its designated Agents may publish updated versions of this License. You may use any authorized version of this License to copy, modify and distribute any Open Game Content originally distributed under any version of this License.

10. Copy of this License: You MUST include a copy of this License with every copy of the Open Game Content You Distribute.

11. Use of Contributor Credits: You may not market or advertise the Open Game Content using the name of any Contributor unless You have written permission from the Contributor to do so.

12. Inability to Comply: If it is impossible for You to comply with any of the terms of this License with respect to some or all of the Open Game Content due to statute, judicial order, or governmental regulation then You may not Use any Open Game Material so affected.

13. Termination: This License will terminate automatically if You fail to comply with all terms herein and fail to cure such breach within 30 days of becoming aware of the breach. All sublicenses shall survive the termination of this License.

14. Reformation: If any provision of this License is held to be unenforceable, such provision shall be reformed only to the extent necessary to make it enforceable.

15. COPYRIGHT NOTICE

Open Game License v 1.0a Copyright 2000, Wizards of the Coast, Inc.

System Reference Document Copyright 2000-2003, Wizards of the Coast, Inc.; Authors Jonathan Tweet, Monte Cook, Skip Williams, Rich Baker, Andy Collins, David Noonan, Rich Redman, Bruce R. Cordell, John D. Rateliff, Thomas Reid, James Wyatt, based on original material by E. Gary Gygax and Dave Arneson.

Swords & Wizardry Core Rules, Copyright 2008, Matthew J. Finch

Monster Compendium: 0e, Copyright 2008, Matthew J. Finch

Sword & Wizardry Complete Rules, Copyright, 2010, Matthew J. Finch

Angel, Monadic Deva, from the *Tome of Horrors Complete,* Copyright 2011, Necromancer Games, Inc., published and distributed by Frog God Games; Author Scott Greene, based on original material by Gary Gygax.

Hex Crawl Chronicles: The Pirate Coast, Copyright 2012, Author John Stater.

www.ingramcontent.com/pod-product-compliance
Lightning Source LLC
Chambersburg PA
CBHW081329090726
47907CB00010B/2422